Rebellion

Ancient Blood
Book Two

by Kristina Bak

ISBN: 978-1-7332747-5-3 (paperback)
ISBN: 978-1-7332747-4-6 (ebook)

For my Critique Partners,

I've learned so much from your advice
and I love the memories we've created.

Thank you for being awesome people
and writers!

Chapter One

Lexy Greggs stared at the three silver stars of insignia as they reflected the light pouring into Ameran's office, the head of the Capital Transport Agency or CTA. A soft layer of dust coated the glass that protected the insignia. Three stars was the top rank a Captain could get. Lexy pulled her sleeve over her hand and wiped the dust away. Her mother's image smiled at her, causing Lexy's heart to ache. She was sixteen when her parents died in an attack on their ship, and ever since the funeral, her mother's stars hung on the wall behind Ameran's desk.

Lexy began to pace in front of the wall-to-ceiling windows.

"Lex, stop. You're worrying over nothing," Zephla, or Z as everyone called him, said his feet propped up on the desk. Ameran hated when he did that. Z was a gray alien and they had a special skill for pissing people off.

"It's not like we've ever gotten good news when she calls us to her office, Lexy said, "I keep running through our missions for the past month. I can't think of anything we messed up." She stopped pacing and glared at Z. They had been best friends their whole life, and he was the biggest troublemaker she knew. "Is there anything I should know about? Did you fuck something up?"

Trent, the head of security, sat in the chair next to Z and chuckled.

Z looked from Lexy to Trent in fake shock, "How dare you accuse me of doing something to damage our chances of getting normal missions again. Do you think I enjoyed cleaning out the cargo bay after that last shipment of pigs from Beta Leo? Honestly."

Lexy shook her head and began pacing again.

Trent shifted to lean his elbows on his thighs, "Lexy, I don't think she called us here for bad news."

Z beamed at Lexy.

"However," Trent continued, "is there anything you need to tell us, Z?"

"Oh, come on. Do you really not trust me?"

"No," both Lexy and Trent responded.

"Whatever," Z scuffed.

Z's small gray form slumped in the chair. He began mumbling under his breath. Lexy rolled her eyes and paced. She had been walking on eggshells for the past month, and her gut twisted every time she thought about the stress she brought on Ameran. The woman was her mother's best friend and looked after Lexy as much as possible without it looking like favoritism. She hated that Ameran and the CTA were now under close watch by the Council and the Royal families.

All because a spoiled King got himself kidnapped on her mission.

Woosh.

Lexy spun on her heel, barely keeping her balance, but restarted her pacing when a short brown and gray reptilian breed brought in a tray of tea and water.

"Director Ameran is on her way. Would you like any refreshment while you wait?" he asked.

Lexy shook her head before stopping to look out the window at the CTA docks below.

Z jumped out of the chair and walked over to the tray. "Do you have anything a little stronger?"

The reptilian sneered, "No."

Z sighed. "I keep telling Ameran she needs to get some better options. Not all of us can be stuffy saints like this guy." He jabbed his thumb at the reptilian, who hissed in response.

Trent stood. "I'm sorry about our pilot's comments. He is just a bit tired and antsy. Would you happen to know if we will have to wait much longer?"

The reptilian's mouth twitched upwards into a shy smile. "Yes, it should be just moments."

"Could I get a cup of tea?" Trent flashed his pearly whites, and Lexy snorted under her breath. The reptilian went straight to work pouring and asking how he took his tea. Once he was finished, the reptilian left the tray and hurried out of the room.

Trent's ability to charm any being he came across still amazed her. He was new to the concept of alien life. A month ago, he was just another ignorant Earthling going about his business until he dove aboard the *Khunda*'s jump ship to save Lexy from danger. Little did he know it was her ship. In just a

Extraterrestrial Response Unit, also known as the Men in Black, getting any information out of him.

They're dumbasses.

The door slid open again, and Ameran, a tall thin woman with blue skin, walked in, followed by a dark-skinned man with gills.

He must be one of the hybrid species the grays created before the war.

Lexy stepped forward, "Director, it's a pleasure to see you again."

The formality felt odd to her, but she knew it was needed if the man accompanying her was there to keep an eye on things.

Ameran nodded coldly, causing Lexy's stomach to twist.

"Captain Lexy Greggs, this is Claes of Polemis, a new member of the Council."

Shit.

Lexy's face must have dropped because Claes waved his hand, "I am not that kind of Council member. I am in training, if you will."

Ameran stepped behind her desk as Lexy shook Claes' smooth hand. The texture reminded her of petting a dolphin.

"Polemis. Isn't that one of the Gray planets? I didn't realize you had representation on the Council." Lexy asked.

Trent pushed another chair to Ameran's desk and motioned for Claes to take it. Lexy stood next to the chair Z had already taken, and he was examining an artifact taken from a nearby shelf.

"Yes," Claes answered, sitting, "I was allowed to sit in on Council meetings for the last four years as a trial run. This is my first year as an official member."

Lexy nodded in understanding. Many of the enlightened species didn't view the Gray planets with respect. So, Lexy was happy to hear they were allowed some representation on the Council.

"Captain Greggs," Claes went on, "when I was alerted to this case, I read up on your history, and first, I would like to express my thanks for your parents and their devotion to the CTA and protecting their cargo. Because of them, a great scientist is alive."

Z huffed, and Lexy glared at him before responding.

"Thank you for that. I assure you that I take my parent's sacrifice seriously."

Ameran nodded, "I explained this to Council member Claes, but he is here for a more important reason. The council has called the crew of *Khunda* for questioning about the events of the Alpha Virgo royal mission."

Z dropped the artifact in his lap, "I thought we were moving on from that?" he asked, his voice an octave higher than usual.

Lexy took the artifact from his hand and placed it on Ameran's desk, "I'm sorry, but I'm not sure why we are being called in for questioning. We filed our reports in accordance with the Royal Guard's guidelines, and Edward-," Lexy took a breath, "I mean, King Edward praised the CTA for our rescue of him from Adohan's ship in his coronation speech. We did everything we could to complete the mission. I'm not sure what other questions they could have. What are they looking for?"

Claes glanced at Ameran before responding.

"Some members of the Council have been pushing for a vote on the gray planets."

"Why? The Gray planets have been in the courts for centuries, so, why would they want to push through a vote now?" Lexy crossed her arms, "And the newsfeeds haven't said anything about it. Wouldn't this be front-page news?"

"The members have wanted to keep it quiet until they know if it will happen. They are worried that the news of a vote could cause an increase in attacks by the rebels." Claes responded, not making eye contact with her.

"Do you have any idea which way the vote could go?" Trent asked.

Ameran took a deep breath.

"That bad, huh?" Z huffed.

"Unfortunately, over the last few years, members of the two enlightened gray planets have joined with the rebellion. Three Royals were assassinated in the last year. And in some of the council member's eyes, your Royal mission was just another sign that the Gray planets were a mistake."

"That wasn't us. We were betrayed." Lexy spat.

Ameran cleared her throat, "We know that, but Apaleo was from a Gray planet."

Silence fell over them.

Trent rested his elbows on his knees. "They feel threatened by the rebellion." His voice sounded strained, as if he just realized Earth's future was on the chopping block because of the choices made by beings light-years away. "They can't wipe out three planets because of the actions of a few," Trent said, more to himself than to the group.

Claes shifted to look at Trent, "They can and they will. The rebellion's numbers are growing, and some members of the Council feel that the Royal system is being threatened." He turned back to face Lexy, "you must not have heard."

Her gut twisted at the tone in his voice.

"A Royal was captured, tortured, and killed on a live feed two days ago."

Lexy dropped to sit on the arm of Z's chair, her hand over her mouth.

Z's voice sounded far off as Lexy's mind raced, "Couldn't they stop the damn feed?"

Claes sighed, "No, the encryption was impenetrable. They must have some new techs on their side."

Ameran was staring out of the window, "The worst part is that they mentioned Apaleo."

"Fuck," Z threw up his hands, "I knew that dick would come back to bite us in the ass."

Ameran's eyes narrowed at Z, "Don't let Zephla talk at your questioning."

"Hey...no, never mind. That's probably a good idea." Z settled back in the chair.

Lexy glanced at her mother's stars, her jaw clenched. Unable to calm her frustration, she looked at Trent, who rubbed the stubble that Z had told him would get him chicks. His eyes connected with hers. She knew he was just as worried. His arms flexed as he rubbed his hands together. His eyebrow raised, letting her know he was with her. Lexy already knew Z was ride-or-die, but she looked at him to see his reaction. He was staring at his shoes. She knew Z was still upset that he didn't see Apaleo's betrayal coming, and felt guilty. The same guilt she felt even though she knew it wasn't her fault. Lexy placed her hand on his shoulder. He looked up at her and shrugged.

Lexy took a deep breath and stood, adjusting her CTA jacket. "I assume Council member Claes is here to inform us of the questioning, officially, " Claes nodded, "And I also assume we cannot reject the Council's request."

He shook his head.

Ameran cleared her throat, "You wouldn't want to try, either."

"Why the fuck not?" Z mumbled.

Claes chuckled. Ameran shifted on her chair.

"Because they will freeze all of your assets. Khunda included. You would not be allowed to work for any company while you stand your ground in protest, and oh yeah, they will put you in jail." Ameran laced her thin blue fingers, resting them on her lip, and narrowed her eyes at Z.

He rolled his eyes, "Oh, that's all."

Lexy looked from Claes to Ameran. It was the first time she noticed a small section of Ameran's black hair had escaped her tight bun. Lexy scanned her face picking up on small details she had overlooked. Her eyes were red around the edges, and the crease between her eyebrows looked a little deeper. Lexy realized that she was dealing with more than she was letting on. Shifting her focus back to Claes, Lexy lifted her chin higher.

"When is the questioning?"

Claes stood, his face unreadable.

Shit, this can't be good.

"Captain Greggs of the class A transport ship, Khunda, you are being summoned to the Council chambers for questioning. Do you have anything to say?"

Lexy extended her wrists toward him, "No."

Claes wrapped a thin silver band around each wrist. The metal was cool and light. It was designed to subdue and track a prisoner without bringing any unwanted attention. Trent jumped out of his chair, his hand reaching out to stop Claes. His face reminded her of a lion protecting the pride. Ameran's light touch made him pause. She shook her head, letting her hand slide off his shoulder.

"Wait, we're doing this shit now?" Z questioned.

Ameran rubbed her temples, "I thought you weren't going to talk until after the questioning?"

"Do you know me?" Z's large eyes looked at each of them, "No, really, does she know who she is talking to?"

Lexy rolled her eyes, "He will do his best, ma'am."

Z stood next to Lexy, his gray arms extended, "I assume that means the whole crew is invited?"

Claes nodded and wrapped a pair of bands on Z's wrists. Then, he turned to Trent, "As head of security, do you have any objections?"

With one last glance at Ameran, Trent held out his wrists, "No, sir."

Lexy rubbed the lightweight bracelets, smiling at Trent. His lips pulled into a tight smile. Her gut tightened, making her wish she hadn't eaten so much at lunch. Being questioned by the council wasn't what she had hoped the meeting would be about, but life has ways of kicking you in the ass.

Claes turned to Ameran, "I will bring them back as soon as the questioning is over."

"Thank you, Claes. I hope they cooperate and keep the profanity to a minimum." She looked at Z, who shrugged.

"I make no promises."

Lexy loved his smart-ass comments, but she hoped he would control himself for once in his life. Claes motioned for Lexy to go first. She took one last glance at Ameran, who was leaning against her desk with her arms crossed. Her face resembled Aunt May's when Lexy left for her service in the Royal Guard. She must be worried about the outcome.

They walked in silence. Beings walked past them, glancing at the silver bands. Lexy pulled her sleeves down. As they walked through the CTA's doors, two beings, a plant crossbreeds by the look of them, began whispering to each other. News of the questioning must have spread further than

Ameran's office. Maybe there was a mole in the Council's chambers. They walked down to the docks, the sun shining. It was a typically perfect day on Alpha Orion. There were only two seasons here, and they were at the end of the longest spring-like season.

Lexy scanned the city skyline. Tall silver buildings scattered the main island like crystals growing in a cave. Small crafts weaved through the buildings, reflecting the few clouds that dotted the sky. Even across the water, Lexy could see the blue haze of the fountains that circled the city. Each of them connected to underground aquatic tunnels for gilled species to use.

Claes stopped at the end of the dock next to a small shuttle, and he held out his hand to help Lexy in. She gave him a small smile and let him help her. She eased herself into the seat next to the steering controls. As the others climbed aboard, she looked over her shoulder at Khunda, one dock over. The large ship hovered silently above the water. She wiped away a tear as Claes started the engine, and they headed toward the Council building in the center of the main island.

Chapter Two

Just outside the Council chambers, one long window took up the wall to the left, while the wall to the right displayed artifacts from the twelve original Enlightened planets.

Claes had left them at the end of this hall, just outside a set of decorated, gold doors depicting the history of the Gray war.

The smooth surface conflicted with the grim images of humanoids floating, dead in space. Other images showed the Grays enslaving them from the Gray planets, Earth included, and taken to the frontlines to fight in the Gray army and inevitably die. Spread across the top of the doors was a depiction of the original Royal families standing on the ruins of a Gray genetics lab. Their success in the war secured their place as the ruling class. The Royals now trained their children to rule over each of the Enlightened planets so any one ideology could not corrupt the political system.

"Permission to speak, Captain," Z said mockingly.

"Permission granted," Lexy sighed, pinching the bridge of her nose.

"Did either of you know they let a Gray planet have representation in the Council?"

Trent leaned against the wall, crossing his arms.

"I did. They mentioned it in one of the training courses I came back for. Though the being that taught the class said it with a bit of disdain. So, I don't know how "enlightened" everyone's being about it."

Lexy looked out over the city. Sleek crafts glided by the window, carrying passengers to various events. She could see the CTA headquarters from this height, although it looked like a blur of green and silver surrounded by crystal blue water.

"Out here is the same as on Earth. Everyone has their own bias, and you're never going to change that. Ameran has always tried to include beings that aren't widely accepted, but she catches a lot of crap for it too." She glanced at Z to see how her comment landed.

He nodded in agreement.

"After the Gray War, several planets closed their ports to us. Some tried to have us killed. Some settled with torturing as many of us as they could catch." He paused looking out the window, "Not all of us believed in the war. Some of us still don't think we should be altering genetics even if it is for the Royals or the Council. However, Ameran's family gave some of us jobs and helped us recover from the backlash."

Trent scratched the back of his neck, "The markings on Lo, was he tortured?"

Lexy and Z both looked at Trent in shock. Lo was the cargo master for the CTA, and he was their go-to guy for anything they needed for missions. Trent must have noticed what Lo tried hard to keep hidden.

Z was the first to talk, "Yes. Not all of us were lucky enough to have friends that stepped up after the war."

Lexy knew he was talking about his great-grandfather, who was friends with Ameran's family during the war. Trent looked at Z in a way that told Lexy he hadn't confided in Trent. Not enough to tell him about his family's history.

One of the doors opened, and a mermaid- human hybrid walked out. A shell held back her long purple hair, but a few curly strands had escaped.

"The Council will see you now." She said.

Her voice was soft like a wind chime and made Lexy want to follow the woman anywhere. But, shaking her head, Lexy thought twice about the woman's mix.

Nope. Not a mermaid. That's a siren.

Lexy looked at the boys, who were both staring. She snapped her fingers in the air.

"Come on, guys. Show some restraint."

Z and Trent shook their heads and followed her through the doors. They walked into a circular room. Chairs, grouped in threes, outlined the room, each row a little higher than the one before. The intention was clearly to make the subject in the center feel small. In each chair sat a member of the Council, all representing several of the thousands of beings from Enlightened planets.

The siren led them to the center of the room, where the Royal symbol was engraved, a sword placed diagonally through a crown. Once in the center, a female that looked to be of Nordic breed stood to address the room.

"Now for file G-132. The issue of the Central Transport Agency's missing Security Officer. Would the witnesses please state their name and rank?"

Lexy straightened.

"Two-Star Captain Lexy Greggs of the Transport ship I."

"Level four pilot Zephla of the Transport ship *Khunda*."

"Head of Security Brandon Trent aboard the Transport ship *Khunda*."

The woman swiped the screen on her ComBoard, making a life-sized hologram of Apaleo float in front of them. Anger boiled up from deep within Lexy's belly. She took a deep breath in an attempt to calm herself.

"This is former top security officer, Apaleo of the Black Mountain tribe on Polemis. He fed a ship of mercenaries information about the transport of King Edward of Alpha Virgo. Then turned on his crew, the crew of *Khunda*, causing a rescue mission led by Captain Marcus Zetha of the transport ship Wonder."

A knot started to form in Lexy's heart at the mention of Marcus' name. She avoided him at all costs since he dropped them off at Khunda. Having been rescued by her cheating ex didn't sit well with her. What made it worse was that she couldn't shake the feelings she still had for him. She dug her nails into her palms, annoyed that he could still get her hot and bothered.

"Although the details of what happened are still unknown, I am assuming that is how Director Ameran wanted it, we will be discussing the possibility that the Central Transport Agency has been compromised and infiltrated by the rebels."

Lexy's eyes widened, unable to hide her shock that the Council would be so open about their intentions.

A blue being sitting next to the lady speaking raised its hand.

"Excuse me madam Speaker, but we should also add that a mid-level Royal was captured and killed after the criminal, Apaleo, escaped the Agency's watch."

Lexy raised her hand.

"I'm sorry, but-"

The Speaker narrowed her eyes at Lexy.

"You will have your time to speak when asked," She hissed.

Lexy glanced at Trent whose face reflected the heat boiling up inside her.

"As I was saying," the Speaker continued, "the Agency's inability to vet their staff led to the near capture and death of another Royal-"

"Madam Speaker, I just-"

The Speaker crossed her arms.

"MISS Greggs. If you cannot contain your outbursts you will have to be removed."

Z pushed his way in front of Lexy.

"Look lady, you are rambling off a whole lot of BS and if any of you want to hear the truth about what happened on that mission then let those of us who were actually there speak," He looked up at Lexy shrugging, "Hey, no one cares if I get removed."

Lexy put her hand on his shoulder.

"I do," she looked up at the Speaker, "I stand by my pilot. Will you let us speak?"

A murmur grew from the rest of the Council. The Speaker glanced around the room. Her eyes twitched and her cheeks flushed red.

"You have the floor, Captain." Her voice full of acid.

Lexy nodded.

"Thank you, Speaker. During that mission, as King Edward has been very open about, he blackmailed us into taking him to a gambling planet. Apaleo quickly agreed, too quickly. And as Captain, I should have noticed but I was worried about the future of my whole crew. We went to the planet not knowing that Apaleo had given our location to the mercenaries led by Captain Adohan. While on the planet we were attacked by Adohan and his crew. From that point on we did what we needed to do in order to save the life of a King. If that doesn't show you how dedicated we and the CTA are to the protection of the Royals then nothing will."

Lexy took a breath.

The room filled with whispers.

She shifted her weight. Her speech began to replay in her head.

Did I say too much? Maybe I should have rephrased it? Did I insult her?

The Speaker raised her hand to silence the room.

"I will now open the floor for questions."

The first Council member to stand was an aqua breed. He was tall with blue skin. Gills waved open and closed on the sides of his neck.

"Apaleo was a member of your crew, correct?"

"Yes," Lexy answered.

"As a member of your crew did you ever have any doubts about his loyalties?"

"I never saw any behaviors that made me question his motives. He was also a temporary member of my crew. He was only assigned to Khunda when our missions required security."

An elf breed stood up behind them. His pale skin reminded Lexy of a storybook vampire.

"You didn't have full-time security on your ship?"

Lexy turned to face him.

"No. The CTA has a hard time finding and keeping security officers because of the dangerous nature of the job. Most of our officers are from Polemis, because they, as you know, are raised to be security for the Royals. Many that I know retire or leave the agency because they have families. And no one wants to leave their family every day wondering if they will ever come home."

A Gray on the other side of the room stood next.

"Does the agency not give them adequate compensation?"

Lexy whipped around to face the new questioner.

"Of course they do, but it's not about money. Every year the number of attacks on Royal ships goes up. What happens when children are left without a parent or both parents?"

She looked at her hands, while the room filled with whispers again. They were talking about her parents, they were whispering about her. When Lexy's parents refused to give up their cargo mercenaries killed them and the rest of their crew. Lexy lost both of her parent's and Z lost his father.

The Speaker stood, causing the room to fall silent once more. Her arrogance floated around her like an aura, dark and smutty.

"As the Captain of your ship, is it not true that you are responsible for the actions of your crew members? We have reports of your crew," she cleared her throat, "fraternizing with the King and each other, Fights among them, and there are even whispers that your current head of security was a stowaway from Earth that only gained his title in an effort to cover up your mistake." She spat the last part at Lexy.

She really didn't like this woman.

"Director Ameran gave him the position because not only was he fully qualified but he proved himself worthy while stepping up to take Apaleo's position when we were betrayed."

Her palms started to burn. Lexy released her fists.

"As for it being my responsibility. Do I wish I had seen something that made me suspicious? Yes, but I didn't see anything. Nothing seemed out of place with Apaleo. He never once showed any sign that he wasn't loyal. I wish I could find him and question him to understand why he did what he did."

A smile spread across the Speaker's face.

Crap.

"Then it is settled. The crew of the Khunda will find Apaleo and bring him back here to face his actions."

Shit. Shit. Shit.

"No, madam Speaker that's not what I meant. I just meant that I wish I could. Not that I would. I have no way of knowing where to find him or even where to start."

The members of the Council began shifting in their seats and whispering among themselves.

"You said you wanted to find him and have him answer for his crimes and so he shall. And who better to bring him in other than the crew that he betrayed. As for where to start, why don't you try asking the man whom he betrayed you for."

With that, the Speaker sat back in her chair.

"You may leave now," she said, waving her hand in the air at them.

Lexy was stunned. Her head spun as the siren that walked them in was now trying to herd them out. How had that happened so quickly? Lexy wasn't the only one in shock. Trent's head was swinging from side to side, his eyes searching for some answers. Z's face was unreadable. He stared straight ahead. No one said anything until they were back in the hall. Trent broke the silence.

"What just happened?"

Z ran his hands down his face.

"I think we just played into that woman's hands. I thought they were supposed to be unbiased."

Lexy shook her head.

"None of that was unbiased. She had an agenda."

Lexy laced her hands behind her neck, breathing into the stretch. Ameran is going to kill me. She jumped as Claes stepped into the hall.

"That could have gone worse."

Z narrowed his eyes at Claes, "Really? How?"

Lexy rubbed the silver band on her wrists.

"I did my best. I didn't know her plan until it was too late," She looked down the hall, "I'll talk to Ameran. Maybe she can talk to the Council. I remember her father had some connections -"

"That won't be necessary," Claes interrupted, "They won't budge on this and this might actually help the Gray planets."

Trent rubbed his forehead. "How? The whole Guard has been on the lookout for Apaleo since he went into hiding. How are we supposed to find him?"

Claes turned and walked down the hallway toward the tubes.

"I'll take you back to your ship."

Lexy followed him, while Z and Trent exchanged looks.

"Come on guys. Let's get back to Khunda so we can talk about what to do next."

Chapter Three

Once onboard Khunda, Claes removed the silver bands from their wrists. Lexy offered him a cup of tea which he accepted. They were all sitting around a table in the common room with a pot of hot water, a selection of teas, and four mugs.

Lexy poured the water into each mug. "Okay, we can talk openly here. Sugar?"

Trent and Z shifted in understanding.

"You think they were listening to us in the hall?" Z asked, "Nosey bastards."

Claes accepted the sugar bowl from Lexy.

"I know they were," he scooped two spoonfuls into his tea, "I have been aware of the Madam Speaker's agenda for some time, but I never thought she would be able to push forward with something so controversial until this last kidnapping. But now she has the leverage to either push a vote through or, as is the case, get you to do the work for her. I didn't want anyone to hear this next part."

He paused looking around the empty room.

"There were a few survivors of the last land attack by the rebels. A small village in the Virgo constellation. The survivors claimed the men who attacked them used Guard-issued weapons and several of them had Guard tattoos on their forearms. Their claims have been silenced since their questioning."

Z poured honey into his mug.

"Why would they do that? Wouldn't the Council want to know if members of the Guard were attacking civilians?"

Claes sipped his tea and set his mug softly on the table.

"That is the question I have been asking since I heard about the claims, but I have been stonewalled. Senior members of the Council have warned me not to step outside my duty since my placement is new and can easily be taken away. So many of us have fought for years for the Gray planets to have representation. If I am kicked off the Council I don't know if we will ever see representation again."

His words hung in the air as they all sipped their tea. The first one to break the silence was Z. He walked to a drawer behind the kitchen counter and pulled out a bottle filled with amber liquid.

"The chief from the Royal mission left this behind so I figure it's fair game," he explained, offering to pour some in Claes' mug, "It's a homemade liquor and a good one at that."

Claes pushed his mug toward Z.

"A little wouldn't hurt."

Trent and Lexy declined the offer, while Z filled his cup.

Claes emptied his mug.

"That is good," he said, his eyes wide, "Madam Speaker did have one good piece of advice. Maybe you should ask the man he betrayed you for."

Lexy was trying to ignore that point.

Claes stood.

"I must get back or rumors may begin to circulate." He nodded at Z, "Thank you for the drink," Then to Trent and Lexy, "It was nice to meet you, and good luck."

With that, he walked back to the elevator and disappeared inside.

Z swung his leg onto the table.

"I like him."

Chapter Four

An hour later they all sat sulking in Ameran's office as she paced behind her desk.

"How could they put this off on you? It is the Guard's responsibility to find fugitives."

Lexy decided against telling her what Claes had told them. There was no way she wanted to be responsible for that reaction.

Trent leaned forward in his chair. "I agree with you that we shouldn't be in this position but since we are, I think that we can do it," He faced Lexy. Maybe in hopes of getting support from her, but that wasn't going to happen. "I don't think it will be easy but Adohan might trade some information if he thinks it could lessen his sentence and civilians wouldn't want to get on the bad side of the Council. So if we can find someone who knows where he is hiding, maybe we can catch a break."

Z snorted. "When have we ever caught a break, newbie?"

Trent dropped back into his chair.

"Just trying to bring a little positivity." He mumbled.

Lexy continued to pick at a string on her cuff. She hadn't noticed Ameran had stopped pacing and was standing with her arms crossed. "Lexy, you don't have to do this."

Lexy let the air out of her lungs, pulling herself to sit up straight.

"No, if we back out now they will have that much more leverage to sway the ruling their way and the Gray planets will be in jeopardy. We have to do everything we can to find Apaleo."

Ameran came to sit on the edge of her desk in front of Lexy.

"You don't have to talk to Adohan. Just let him rot in jail."

Lexy shook her head. "No, I have to. He's our best chance. Without him, we will have no idea where to start."

Ameran sighed. "Fine, but at least don't go alone."

"I'll go with her," Trent said, "I would love to see that SOB behind bars." He leaned back in his chair, lacing his fingers behind his head and arched back. Lexy noticed a tattoo just above his elbow. She couldn't make out what it was, but it made her want to ask him about it. Just another thing to add to her to do list once she fixed the mess they were in.

Ameran looked at all three of them, then stood and walked to the other side of her desk.

"If you're doing this then I'm sending you with some help."

Lexy began to protest but decided against it when she noticed the force with which Ameran was typing.

"Ali can help you with any cultural and technical needs," She explained still typing just a little too hard.

Lexy didn't disagree with Ali joining them. She was one of the best engineers and the Council often used her to help transition newly enlightened planets. She would be an asset.

"And Captain Zetha has connections everywhere, so maybe he can keep you three out of too much trouble."

Lexy stood at the mention of Marcus. "Director, I don't think we need Marcu- I mean Captain Zetha. Is there anyone else you can think of? Like anyone. Anyone at all?"

Ameran looked up at Lexy. Her dark eyes narrowed in thought, the blue skin between hert eyebrows pinching.

Good, she's thinking of someone else.

"No."

Dammit.

"Captain Zetha is your best choice." Ameran looked back at her screen.

Z groaned and let his head fall back. "Well, this just got worse."

Ameran finished typing. "I have ordered you a week's worth of supplies. I hope it won't take that long but if it does you can always come back for more. If you get into trouble don't hesitate to call the Guard or other CTA ships. When you get him, lock him up and don't interact with him. Apaleo is a skilled fighter but he was one of our best at manipulation."

Lexy looked at Trent questioningly. Trent shrugged, he of all of them had spent the least amount of time with Apaleo, but maybe boys talk about these things, right? Like my Jedi-mind-tricks are better than your Jedi-mind-tricks.

Z laughed. "Yeah, once I saw him talk a gypsy breed into buying him a drink. And those guys are the ones always trying to get you to buy them one."

Trent looked at Z.

"When did you go out drinking with Apaleo?"

Z shook his head. "Oh, I didn't. I was just at the same bar. That man has the personality of a rock. No way I would've hung out with him."

Ameran squinted at Z before continuing to type.

"I will have Lo pull some extra boxes for you. If you need anything else just ask him."

Ameran finished entering the orders and stood with her hands on her waist. Looking at each of them. Her eyes stopped on Lexy. "Well you better get going, you have a lot of supplies to load up." Her voice was tight.

Lexy walked over to Ameran and wrapped her arms around her thin frame. "We'll be fine."

Ameran returned the hug for a second before letting go. She never was very sentimental. Lexy figured it had to do with her relationship with her father. Lexy had only met him once but he was cold toward his daughter. He didn't show her any affection, and he hardly even made eye contact.

Lexy turned to leave, while Trent and Z both stood to follow her thanking Ameran as they did.

They entered the tube just outside the office. Lexy watched Ameran as the tube descended. She was organizing the folders, but Lexy knew it was to cover up the tears falling onto her desk.

Lexy's gut twisted as the tube came to a stop on the supply floor. Z was talking, but she wasn't listening. Her thoughts were bouncing between lists of needed supplies to questioning how she was going to avoid Marcus while they were on the same ship.

Lo was in the stacks when they arrived. Lexy leaned over the glass console and started searching through the catalogs. Trent stood next to her opening the security catalog and flipping through the choices.

"You okay?" He asked nonchalantly.

Z pushed a stool up to Lexy's other side. "How would you be if you were going to be stuck on a ship with your ex, the fate of your planet landed on your to-do list, and you had to face the man that tortured you?" Lexy glared at him. "What? I'm right though."

She went back to flipping through medical supplies. "Z, we really need to have a talk about your lack of filter."

He shrugged and started flipping through the food catalog.

Lo returned from the stacks, his body shape similar to Z's except his skin was a darker shade of gray and scars peeked from under his collar, he was typing away on his ComBoard. "Hey, guys. I hear you told the Council you would hunt down the traitor for them. That's so nice of you." He smiled sarcastically.

"Damn, word travels fast," Z said, looking up from the screen.

Lo stepped onto another stool and fist-bumped Z then nodded to Trent. "What's up, newbie?"

"Not much," Trent mumbled back.

"Lo, do you have any suggestions for anything we may have missed?" Lexy asked him while flipping through the tech catalog. She had no idea what they would need.

Lo leaned across the console, resting his chin on his palm.

"Lexy, my dear favorite Captain, do you really think that I wouldn't have the hook up for you?"

Lexy shrugged. She knew that Lo was held in high respect by most of the beings that worked at the CTA. She always wondered if it was because of what happened to him in the war or maybe there was something she, as an Earthling, wasn't privy to.

"I already sent you a custom box full of goodies that were hand chosen, by yours truly."

"Oh, thanks." Lexy went back to the catalogs.

Lo exchanged looks with Z. "Did I miss something? Why so somber?"

Z threw up his hands. "I'm not saying. Apparently, I have no filter."

Lexy rolled her eyes. She would have thought after being friends with Z all of her life she would be used to his sass by now.

"Our first stop is to talk with Adohan," Trent explained.

Lo's eyes widened in understanding. "Ooooooooh, that suuuuuuuucks. Are you okay with that, Lex?"

"I have to be. There isn't a better choice." She took a deep breath in an effort to relax her muscles.

Lo picked up his ComBoard and started typing. "When you see him be sure to give him a nut shot for me."

Lexy laughed. "Deal."

Back on Khunda, they were unpacking their orders when Ali arrived. Lexy grunted and cursed as she tried to push a large metal crate into the corner of the cargo bay.

"Stupid…who packs this shit…fuuuuu…"

"Does your aunt know you talk like that?" Ali's soft tone calmed Lexy's frayed nerves.

She whipped around, Ali walked up the ramp with her long blond hair braided, showing off her pointed ears. She was wearing a flowing dress and as always she looked like an angel. This made sense because Earth's history was riddled with stories of angels that were simply Elf-bred aliens. Ali was holding a duffle bag with the CTA logo on the front and a messenger bag hanging on her shoulder.

Lexy ran up to her, throwing her arms around Ali's neck.

"It's so good to see you. How have you been? Where have you been?"

Ali hugged her back.

"I've been out in the Gemini constellation helping to rebuild."

"The Dali Lama was out there the last time I spoke to him," Lexy replied before she could stop herself. She kept forgetting to send him a message. Maybe she did forget, maybe she was afraid of talking to the only person she knew she couldn't lie to. He always had a way of getting the truth out of her.

"I know. I got to spend some time with him. He is the one that told me about how your Royal mission went. Which we need to talk about."

Lexy looked at her feet. Whenever asked about the mission she quickly thought up ways to change the subject. Lucky for her, Trent walked up the ramp carrying a food box.

"Hey Ali, long time no see." Trent set the box on top of the crate Lexy was trying to move. He gave Ali a one-armed hug.

"I see you are being put to use." Ali joked, nodding toward the large supply of crates and boxes in the rear of the cargo bay.

Trent shrugged. "Yeah, I think we over-ordered."

Lexy reached for Ali's duffle bag. "I'll show you to your room." She cut in as Ali gave Trent a flirty smile. She didn't like the way they looked at each other. It made her gut twist.

Z walked out of the elevator just as they walked up to it.

"Hey Ali, are you ready for an adventure?" They high-fived.

"I'm always ready if you're my pilot." Ali laughed.

Lexy led the way into the elevator and pushed the button for the guest floor. The last time that floor was used was by Edward and his staff. The bedrooms were redecorated for that mission, but as soon as they got back to the CTA Lexy had them cleaned up. She wanted her normal guest rooms back.

When the elevator stopped, Lexy waved her arm toward the doors that circled the room. "Your choice."

Ali smiled and chose the second door to the left.

"This was the room I stayed in when we first met. Remember? You were taking me to help set up some new tech at some capital on a small planet."

Lexy laughed. "I remember because that was one of our first missions and I'd never met an elf breed before."

She put Ali's bag on a chair in the corner and peeked in the bathroom to make sure everything was back to normal. The housekeeping crew always did a top job.

Ali slid her bag onto the chair in front of the desk. "Yeah, and you spent half the trip trying to not look at my ears."

They laughed. Ali sat down on the bed, looking at Lexy like she could see straight through her. "Are you sure you're okay?"

Lexy picked at her cuticle. "I'm fine."

Ali patted the bed in front of her.

"'I'm fine.' Doesn't mean you're good. It means you're just getting by. Do you want to talk?"

Lexy flopped face-first onto the bed.

"I don't know," she said into the bedsheet.

Ali rubbed her back.

"From what I was told you have a lot going on."

Lexy shifted to face Ali.

"I guess, but what can I do? Freak out about it? I just have to keep going, right?"

Ali tucked a stray piece of blonde hair behind her ear.

"Yes, but have you talked to anyone?"

"I'm talking to you."

"Okay, am I the only one?"

Lexy sat up tucking her leg underneath her. She thought about the night she got home from the Royal mission. Aunt May brought Bones, Lexy's five-year-old all-black German shepherd, to the home she shared with him and a bag of groceries. She asked Lexy how it went and Lexy's mumbled 'fine' seemed to be enough for her. That night she did tell Bones about it, though.

"Bones is a good listener," Lexy told her, avoiding Ali's eyes.

Ali laughed. "I bet he is, but Lex you can't keep this all to yourself."

Lexy rolled onto her back and started talking. She told Ali about everything. About how that mission was supposed to bring her one step closer to her third captain star, but it took her five steps back, instead. How, then Prince Edward, had cornered her into taking him to the gambling planet and how Apaleo must have sent a message to Adohan about their location. Tears started streaming from Lexy's eyes. She continued on about how Edward was kidnapped and Apaleo tricked her and left her on the mercenary's ship to get her ass kicked. She told Ali about waking up chained to the ceiling and how all she could think was that it was all her fault. Ali stayed silent and Lexy continued filling Ali in on her nightmares and writer's block since that mission. The words continued to pour out of her. Thoughts and feelings she hadn't even told her Aunt about and some she didn't even know she had. When she was done she felt better than she had in weeks.

Ali shifted to face her. "You are the Captain of this ship and your crew needs you to be in a good headspace. They don't want to follow an unstable captain. You have to take care of yourself in order to take care of them."

Lexy nodded, tears drying on her cheeks.

Ali lay on the bed next to her and tilted her head to touch Lexy's. Instantly, Lexy started to feel the stress and anxiety melt away.

"Are you doing elf magic on me?" Lexy asked, enjoying the feeling in her shoulders as they relaxed down her back.

"Yes. Now shhh so I can focus. Then we can go steal some of the food Z ordered."

Lexy smiled. She really did have some of the best friends in the universe.

After all of the crates were put away and Marcus was hiding in his room due to what Lexy assumed were the nasty looks Trent and Z kept giving him, Lexy called a meeting on the bridge to discuss the plan.

"Our first stop is the prison planet, Laki, to question Adohan. He has to know where Apaleo would go into hiding or at least how we can get into contact with him." She paced in front of the console as Ali sat in her chair, Z reclined in his, and Trent searched the navigation screen. Marcus leaned against the door frame, glaring at Z who had called him to the meeting by blaring Britney Spears in his room.

Lexy turned on her heels and continued.

"I ordered a good supply of weapons, half are secured in the cargo bay lock up and the other half I asked Trent to secure in secret locations just in case."

Marcus cut in, "Are you sure that is a good idea? Remember what happened to your last head of security?"

Lexy stopped, her hands landing on her hips. She hoped he wouldn't notice her avoiding making direct eye contact. "This is my ship so no critiques from you."

Marcus huffed, sliding his hands into his pockets. A few loose strands of his brown hair fell over his crystal blue eyes reminding Lexy of that night they were stuck on an outpost together. Her pulse quickened when his biceps flexed against his rolled-up sleeves.

What are you doing? Cheating ex! Remember Lexy.

She glanced at the others, each looking at the main screen where Trent had pulled up Laki and their fastest route.

She crossed her arms and continued. "Like I was saying. We also have a lot of tech that Ali will go through after dinner. Some of this stuff is still under development by the CTA nerds. So don't break it. Take my word for it they may be all about the calming drugs but they will lose their shit if you break the tech. Got it?"

Everyone nodded.

"Extra supplies are on level three. All of the food has been stored in the kitchen. Any questions?"

Z kicked his feet onto the console. "Yeah, I'm missing two boxes of Zebra cakes. Anyone know what happened to them?"

Ali covered a giggle with a fake cough while Lexy fought to hide her smile. "Anyone have any serious questions?"

Z looked suspiciously between Ali and Lexy as Trent raised his hand slowly.

"How are we going to get in to question Adohan?"

Lexy leaned on the console. "Ameran called ahead and pulled some strings. It seems the Council was glad to corner us into finding Apaleo but they forgot to give us top clearance. So Trent and I will be visiting Adohan as his sister and brother-in-law. Ali has been kind enough to create some fake ID chips for us."

Z snorted. "Newbie has to play your husband? Man, I feel bad for you, dude. Lexy would be a horrible wife."

Lexy slapped his feet off the console. "Laki has top-of-the-line security so we won't be able to wear our ComBands. The rest of you are going to wait here. I asked Khunda to search through news feeds from the last week for specific keywords that might help us find Apaleo. You guys can search through those while we're questioning Adohan."

Everyone nodded in acknowledgment.

"Okay, that's all for now. We will leave first thing in the morning."

Marcus took a step toward Lexy making her heart leap and her lower region warm. She froze unsure of how to escape.

Ali stood cutting him off and she looped her arm through Lexy's. "I'm starving. Let's go see what meal packs Z ordered."

"I knew it!" Z yelled after them, "You owe me Zebra cakes!"

Chapter Five

The next morning, Lexy showered and changed into black pants and a long sleeve shirt. She braided her hair, sat on the couch, and tried to type. Nothing. She was still blocked and lacking motivation. Her agent was going to kill her if she didn't start another book, but then again none of that would matter if she couldn't save Earth.

She closed her laptop, plugging it in to charge on the table next to the couch. The journal Edward had given her sat on the opposite corner. Picking it up she flipped through a few pages. The handwriting was elegant and some of the corners had beautiful sketches of flowers. Her finger traced the leaves of a seven-petal one. She didn't recognize the language, though she never claimed to be a linguist. The lines twisted around each other and dots were placed along with them.

It must be very old.

Lexy flipped to the back of the journal and a small lock of hair fell onto her lap. She picked up the ribbon-wrapped dark strands.

That's odd.

Tucking the hair between the pages she placed the book onto the bookshelf and made a mental note to ask Ali about the language when she had some time.

She grabbed a jacket on her way out of the room. Z and Trent's voices floated up from the common room below. Lexy hugged the wall, hoping they wouldn't see her slip onto the bridge.

"Good morning." Marcus's deep voice made her heart skip a beat.

Dammit.

Marcus stood in front of the screen.

"Please don't leave," He pleaded as Lexy turned.

She sighed, resigning herself to the fact that she was going to have to talk to him at some point. No matter how much it messed with her hormones. She turned back to face him, crossing her arms.

"You have until one of the others comes in."

Marcus rubbed his palms together in front of him. "I wanted to tell you that I am going to give you your space until – well if you ever wanted to uh talk or something."

The look in his eyes made her shell crack. There was something there.

Maybe he really has changed. What if he is sorry?

"Okay." was the only word that came to mind.

They stood there, staring at each other. Memories flooded Lexy's mind. The way he always pulled the blanket up to her shoulders because he knew she would get cold. The time he tried to make her dinner, but they ended up feeding each other fruit on the kitchen floor coughing because the smoke was so thick. The memories made her feel the depth of her lonely life without him. She missed the routine they had slipped into in the short time they were together.

Marcus looked as if he was about to step toward her as the door slid open.

"There you are, Lex." Ali stopped at the sight of Marcus. "Oh, sorry. Am I interrupting anything?"

Lexy wiped away a tear before anyone could notice, she stepped up to her console and began typing. "Khunda."

"Yes, captain."

"Can you call the rest of the crew to the bridge and begin final checks before takeoff?"

"Of course, captain. Or as Pilot Zetha says, 'you bet your tight little ass.'"

Lexy dropped her head, she could hear Z laughing through the still-open door.

"I have got to remember to tweak her learning parameters."

After the final checks were done they set out for the prison planet, Laki. The trip only took them two hours. Trent and Ali went to the cargo bay to cover any markings the jump ship had that would give them away as a CTA crew and Lexy stayed on the bridge. Unfortunately, Marcus did too.

This peeved Z, who decided to play twenty questions with Marcus. They were on question fifty.

"Were you dropped as a child?"

Marcus had his hand over his eyes.

"No. Why are you asking me these questions?"

"Just want to get to know you, buddy."

Lexy stood to stretch.

"I'm going to the cargo bay to prep the jump ship."

Marcus looked as if he was going to ask if she needed help but then thought again. As she hurried out, Z began his questions again.

"Do you pee sitting or standing?"

Lexy couldn't help but laugh at that one.

The trip in the jump ship to Laki was a quiet one. Trent was always good about knowing when Lexy was in her head and didn't want to be disturbed. It was one of the traits she liked about him. Talking wasn't a strength of hers, that is why she was a writer. She could edit and review her words until they were what she wanted to say.

They landed the jump ship in front of the entrance. The building was small compared to the massive underground prison Lexy had heard about. The prisoners dug out more sections as part of their sentence. It was dangerous. She had heard several news feeds tell about a tunnel collapsing and killing several prisoners, although they never specified how many.

Lexy would have thought it was a sad way to die except in order to be put in this particular prison you had to have done something really bad. Like horror movie bad.

They walked up to the guard at the door.

"I'm Scarlet. I'm here to visit my brother, Captain Adohan."

The guard was tall and broad shouldered with dark hair. If Lexy had never met one before she would have never known he was a lycan breed. The one detail that gave it away was their teeth. Lycans had slightly longer canines. While working for the Royal Guard she got an up close and personal look at one. She didn't want to have a repeat of that. So she flashed him her sweetest smile.

He checked the list and let out a low grumble.

"Go ahead." He buzzed them through the door.

Inside two guards were sitting behind a table in front of the elevators. Next to them was an archway that glowed soft blue.

Lexy led Trent to the table as one of the guards handed them visitor tags without looking up from his ComBoard. The other pointed them to the archway. Lexy walked through first. The light turned green. Trent followed, another green. They walked to the open elevator and stepped in.

There were no buttons to push but the elevator began to move before they had a chance to question it.

"Was that like a metal detector?" Trent asked.

Lexy shook her head.

"Not really. It's more of an intention detector. If you come here wanting to set someone free then the light turns red and you are detained."

"It can read your thoughts?" He asked, sounding shocked.

She shook her head. "No, it reads body language and vitals. Our bodies tell far more than we know."

Trent shoved his hands into his pockets. "What if you come here with thoughts of harming a prisoner?"

Lexy looked at him to see if he was serious. He was.

"No, they don't care about that. If you want to hurt a prisoner their motto is 'go ahead, they deserve it'"

"Hm, in Adohan's case I could see that. He would deserve it." Trent's voice pulled at Lexy's heart, he really was a natural protector. She was lucky to have him as a friend.

"Yes," she responded, clearing her throat that seemed to get tighter the further down the elevator went, "but we need information from him so no fighting, okay?"

Trent looked at his boots.

"Trent." Her voice was stern.

"Fine. I agree. Take all the fun out of it." He mumbled back.

The doors opened to a sterile hallway. At the end, a lady sat behind a simple black desk. Lexy walked to the front of the desk but before she could open her mouth the lady yelled to the back room.

"PRISONER 522438 TO CUBE THREE!"

Lexy stretched her jaw in an attempt to stop her ear from ringing. She had never heard someone yell that loud before.

"Thank you." Lexy said, just a little too loudly herself.

Trent guided her to cube three, while she cupped her ears. The room had clear walls, a clear table and clear chairs. Nothing could be hidden in here. The table sat in the center of the room with a chain on either side. An extra chair sat in the corner by the door.

"Geeze, how were you not affected by that?"

He pulled the extra chair up to the table. "Years of working in close proximity to jet engines."

Lexy nodded in acknowledgement. The ringing was beginning to subside. She sat in the chair, but Trent remained standing. His eyes followed three men who were walking their way. One of them was Adohan.

Lexy's stomach jumped into her throat. She clenched her jaw in an attempt to keep from vomiting breakfast everywhere.

He looked skinnier and hunched over. His hair was longer and wild. As they walked into the room and he turned to allow the guard to undo his cuffs Lexy thought she saw fresh cuts along his collarbone.

He rubbed his wrists as the guard listed off the rules. Lexy couldn't hear them. She was staring at Adohan's smirk. Anger bubbled up inside of her like hot lava. She could see herself jumping over the table, knocking him to the ground, and punching him over and over. It scared her how much she wanted to hurt him and that she knew she would enjoy seeing him bleed.

The click of the door closing brought her back.

"Well, Captain Greggs. I figured you'd come to see me. Miss me did you?"

"Go to hell," She growled.

He grabbed the back of the chair sliding it to him and taking a seat. He waved his arms.

"Darling, look around. I'm in hell."

Lexy clinched her fists. "You deserve worse."

Adohan laughed, the sound bouncing off the clean walls.

"That's it girl, talk dirty to me. It gets lonely here. I need something to, uh, brighten my day."

He winked at her and before she knew it she'd jumped over the desk and pulled him out of his chair, using her weight to throw him onto the table. Her forearm pressed into his neck.

"We should have killed you when we found you."

"Tisk, tisk," He smiled, "Remember Captain Greggs you didn't find me. Your boyfriend did."

Lexy pushed all of her weight into his neck, his face turning red. He started spitting, trying to gasp for air.

How long would it take for him to lose consciousness?

Trent grabbed a hold of Lexy's shoulder.

She met his eyes.

"Lexy, let go." His even voice brought her back.

She did backing up and straightening her jacket. Trent helped Adohan back into his chair, forcefully. Lexy returned to hers, crossing her arms to hide her shaking hands.

"You know why we're here." She said.

Adohan rubbed his neck.

"Of course I do. I knew it was just a matter of time. Let me guess your doing the Council's dirty work."

Lexy glanced at Trent. There was no way news of their meeting with the Council had reached him already.

"What makes you think the Council sent us?"

He smiled.

"Because Apaleo is a loose string they need to cut before he talks."

Lexy uncrossed her arms, shifting her weight in the chair.

"Talks about what?"

Adohan slouched back in his chair, crossing his arms.

"About secrets."

Trent, still standing next to his chair, nudged Adohan's shoulder.

"How about you elaborate."

Adohan huffed. "The Council isn't innocent. They have a hand in the creation of the rebellion and they even pull some of the strings."

"Bull shit," Lexy snapped, "The Council has been fighting the rebel movement since day one."

Even as she said it she could hear in her voice that she didn't fully believe it. After meeting members of the Council she had her doubts they were all there for the same reasons.

"Thats fine don't believe me, but Apaleo did. Not only did he believe in the movement, he had proof." Adohan was looking around the room, maybe for a way out.

"Proof? If he had proof why wouldn't he come forward or tell someone? Instead he not only teamed up with you but he served me up as dessert."

Adohan pushed back in his chair lifting the front two legs off the ground.

"That my beautiful Captain was my idea. He wasn't very happy about it. But you do what you have to to save your people, I guess. As for the proof. How long do you think he would have lived after sharing that little nugget."

He dropped the front of his chair back on the ground. Leaning forward with his elbows on his knees, he looked Lexy straight in the eyes.

"You do know that he has a family. A tribe. A planet. Right?" He asked in a hushed tone.

Lexy felt her cheeks burning. She had never really thought of Apaleo as ever having a family, but he must have. He had to come from somewhere. Someone. He had to have a mother and father, even a sibling maybe.

"I — I never." Her voice was losing whatever confidence she had.

"You never thought about it did you? You're no better than the rest of the Royal snobs. All you see is your own bubble," He snarled.

Lexy slammed her hand down on the table.

"Hey, I have shit to deal with, too. I'm trying to keep the Council from ruling to destroy the Gray planets. That is a lot of fucking weight to carry."

Oddly she felt better having said it out loud, even if it was to Adohan.

"At least you have a planet to save. Some of us don't get that luxury." He spit back at her, "and I wonder who's responsible for that."

Lexy stared at him questioningly. There were no planets that she knew of that were destroyed within their life time. Especially not by the Counsel. Maybe he just said it for dramatic effect.

Movement out of the corner of her eye caused her to look away from him. A guard walked their way. Adohan shifted in his chair, bringing her attention back to him. She thought she saw a glimmer of fear in his eyes. Lexy knew this was the last chance she may get to ask him.

"Where is Apaleo hiding?"

Adohan stood and Trent walked to stand next to Lexy.

"Where is he?" Lexy asked again.

Adohan touched his wrists in front of him as the guard entered the room.

"Wait," Lexy extended her hand, "Wait, we're not done." Trent was holding her arm keeping her from moving closer. "We didn't call you."

"You're done," The guard sneered at her hand, showing his pointy teeth.

Adohan stared at the top of the guard's head as he cuffed him.

"You know my dear Captain, I always found out about my target before I took a job. Maybe you should do the same. Take Crain here. His husband is cheating on him and he knows it but they stay together for the kids. Which we all know works out every time."

The guard looked at Adohan in shock then punched him in the gut before slamming his head onto the table.

Lexy jumped back in shock as Trent came to stand between her and them. The guard looked up at Lexy. "You're done."

She watched as the guard dragged the half-conscious Adohan out of the room. They both stood there for a few moments after the guard disappeared with Adohan behind a door.

Trent was the first to move.. "We should go," he said leading her back to the elevators.

Chapter Six

Back on *Khunda*, Lexy sat on the bridge with her knees to her chest, sipping tea. The images of what happened on Laki floated around in her head. Trent had just finished filling everyone in. They were all silent as they processed the events.

Z sighed, shifting to cross his thin arms. "At least they're giving him the royal shithead treatment he deserves," Z commented.

Ali was standing next to Lexy, a look of concern on her face.

"Do you think he was trying to help us? I mean, 'maybe you should do the same' sounds like he was trying to help."

Z snorted. "Or maybe he just wanted to take a little stab at the guard. Man, I wish I could have seen him get his ass kicked."

Lexy let her feet drop to the floor. "It's all we have, so maybe we start there and see where it leads."

Marcus, leaning against the door frame, pulled himself upright. "I agree. Khunda, could you pull —"

"What do you think you're doing?" Lexy snapped, "My ship, remember?" Lexy set the cup on the console, "Khunda, please pull all the records you have on Apaleo, former CTA head of security and divide them between each of our comboards."

"Yes, Captain," Khunda responded.

Lexy looked at her comboard as files began sliding across her screen.

"Okay, well, we all have some reading, so let's get to it."

Over the next hour, they all left to find comfy places to read. First, Lexy went to the common room for a snack, reading through several mission files. Then, she stretched out on her couch, reading through a few more. After that, she cuddled up on her bed and read more files. Finally, frustrated, she walked out to the railing above the common room. Z was sipping on a thick purple drink with his comboard propped in front of him. At the table next to Z, Trent sat with his feet on the table, eating chips with his comboard in his lap. Ali was lying on the floor with her legs up the wall, holding her board.

"Does anyone have any info that doesn't pertain to a mission?"

They all looked up at her and then looked at each other.

"That's what I thought," Lexy headed to the elevator, "Khunda, call a meeting in the observation room."

"Yes, Captain."

Khunda's calm voice was the opposite of how Lexy felt. If they only had mission files, there wouldn't be anything about his personal life. Nothing they could use to find out what planet he was from, if he had a family, or what tribe he belonged to. As the elevator slid down a level, she thought about how she had worked next to him for so long and didn't know anything about him. Then, as the door slid open, Marcus's smile greeted her.

Lexy jumped. "Don't fucking do that!" she snapped at him.

"You never used to be so jumpy. What's up?" he asked.

She left the elevator and he fell in step next to her. His cologne mixed with his sweat caused Lexy's cheeks to flush. She remembered that smell from when they would work out together, which often led to them showering together.

Lexy shook the thoughts from her mind.

"Nothing," she grumbled as he held the door to the observation room open for her.

The others were already standing in the curved room, comboards in hand. The window that took up the opposite wall looked out into space. Only darkness and stars were visible from their current position. Z had brought Khunda to float near an uninhabitable planet in hopes that no one, especially the Royal Guard, would bother them.

Setting her comboard on the railing, Lexy stretched her back. "Khunda, please show us all the files on Apaleo."

Holographic files popped up around the room, floating in midair.

"Khunda, please remove all mission files for the CTA."

Half the files disappeared. Lexy walked around, looking at several of the transparent forms.

"Please remove any file that Apaleo authored." She continued.

Only three files were left.

That's annoying.

"Khunda, can you cross-reference these three files to see if there are any keywords that match?"

A list of words popped up in the center of the room. Lexy walked over to it, scrolling through them. One word at the top of the list stood out to her: Aria. The name of a Gray planet. The warrior planet. She squinted, thinking it made sense that Apaleo was from Aria, but she had never thought about it before. Most of the Royal Guard was from there. The humanoids there were genetically made for battle and protection. Apaleo was the best security officer the CTA had. How had she never put the two together?

Lexy pointed to the word.

"There. He has to be there."

They all walked forward-looking at the word.

"Is that his home planet?" Marcus asked.

Lexy shrugged.

"I guess. He never told me which planet he came from and I never asked," she admitted.

"It's worth a try," Trent added.

"But which tribe?" Z asked, "There have to be millions on Aria. That's like going to Earth and walking around London looking for someone when they live in Tokyo."

Z was right. The planet was bigger than Earth, with tribes scattered all over. Lexy began to pace along the railing. Walking always helped her think. If Apaleo was in hiding, he couldn't buy any necessities. All enlightened planets had the same Royal credit system. It was the only way for beings to buy and sell. Of course, thriving illegal trade markets popped up on planets all the time. Z and Lexy had to raid a few while working in the Royal Guard. Even if Apaleo took full advantage of these markets it wouldn't be enough to survive. Someone has to be smuggling for him.

"Khunda, could you check Apaleo's personnel file from the CTA for his person of contact?"

"Wouldn't they have already tried that?" Trent asked.

"Maybe, but Guard members in uniforms would have questioned the contact. People from the warrior planets tend to refuse questioning from the Guard," Lexy explained.

Z laughed. "And Lex would know. When we worked for the Guard, there was this one time —"

Lexy raised her eyebrow at him.

"You know what. That's a story for another time," Z said, raising his hands.

"I found his contact, Captain. It is a Nora of the Utu tribe on the planet Aria," Khunda stated.

Marcus clapped his hands together. "Alright, let's call her up and have a chat."

"No. We are still members of the CTA. She won't talk to us, let alone give up his location. Who knows what relationship she has with Apaleo? She could be a member of his family, or he has something he's holding over her head. Either way, we are only going to get one shot, and we can't fuck it up."

Lexy turned to look out the observation window, resting her elbows on the railing.

How do we play this?

"We need to follow her. See what her daily pattern is. Then two of us can try to question her. She will more than likely refuse, but maybe it will be enough for her to make contact with him."

Ali twirled a strand of her hair. "That's a good idea. I can get a read on her if I can get close enough. Maybe shake her hand or just touch her to get her attention. It would need to be somewhere without a crowd, so I don't pick up on the wrong person. Maybe I can get a sense of if she is afraid of him or loves him."

Lexy nodded. "I think that could work. We are going to have to split into pairs: Marcus, you go with Ali; Trent, you come with me. Z, you hang back on the jump ship in case we need some help."

Lexy pointed her finger at Marcus just as he opened his mouth to protest. "My ship," Lexy snapped. "Z, how long to Aria?"

Z bent over his comboard, typing in the destination. "Looks like twelve hours and two jumps. Most of which will be overnight. So we can prep everything tonight and be ready to go in the morning."

Lexy clapped her hand together. "Alright. In that case, let's get started. Z, set us on course. Trent, can you stock the jump ship with some basic direct energy pistols. If we have to use our weapons, I would rather not make too much noise. And throw some medical supplies onboard too, just in case. Marcus, can you do some research on the Utu tribe's customs so we don't get into any unwanted trouble?"

Z snorted. "Yeah, 'cause that never happens to us."

Lexy pinched the bridge of her nose. "You're not wrong, so I want to be as prepared as possible without setting off any alarms. There will be members of the Guard there to protect any Royal buildings and personnel. And the tribes tend to have their own way of protecting themselves. We can't tip anyone off as to why we're there." She glanced at her ComBand. "Ali, can you take me through the tech Lo gave us? I want every leg up we can get."

Ali nodded.

Lexy's stomach started to twist. She didn't know if it was because of what they were up against or because she hadn't eaten much.

"Lex, might I suggest food first. I know I always work better on a full stomach," Z suggested as if he read her mind.

Lexy smiled. She could always count on Z to make sure they were fed.

"Yes, dinner first, then we prep."

After dinner, Lexy and Ali went to the cargo bay followed by Z once Khunda was on course for Aria.

Ali told Lexy about the ear comms, stun discs, and a handheld body scanner that Z was currently playing with. After telling him several times to stop looking at her, Ali snatched it from him putting it on the highest shelf. Far out of reach for his four-foot-something frame.

"That's just insulting," he groaned.

"You better be glad I didn't slap you." Ali crossed her arms and turned her attention back to the work table covered with tech. Most of which still looked like it was in the development and testing phase.

"Okay, so each of us will get an ear comm. Trent and Marcus can split the stun discs, and Ali will be in control of the body scanner. I think that is all we will take. I don't want to give anyone the wrong idea. Z, since you will be staying on the jump ship, you get a weapon, but I hope you won't need anything else," Lexy said, scanning the tech spread out before her.

Z crossed his arms. "I never get to have fun."

Trent walked up next to Z. "Weren't you the one who suggested the strip joint we were in when Adohan caught up with us? That wasn't fun enough?"

Z faked a shocked look. "I have no idea what you're talking about. I would never suggest such a low-class establishment."

Lexy continued, rubbing the scar on her arm Adohan had given her, "Ali, you and Marcus will follow Nora just close enough to keep an eye on her but not enough to spook her. Trent and I will follow from further behind as backup in case you need it. Let's see how tomorrow goes and play it by ear."

They nodded in response.

Lexy yawned. "I'm going to go to bed, but first, Z, can you take me through our flight plan?"

"Sure. I need a pre-bed snack anyway." He responded, taking one final disappointed glance at the body scanner.

Lexy and Z left Trent and Ali discussing a piece of tech that Ali explained would connect to a being's neural pathways forcing them to tell the truth. Trent listened with intent, and what Lexy thought was a glint in his eyes. She couldn't help but wonder if Trent was hoping for more alone time with Ali. After all, she wasn't just beautiful, she was also the most intelligent person Lexy knew. What man, or woman for that matter, wouldn't be attracted to her? She sighed as Z rambled on about some adjustments he made to Khunda's systems to make it harder for the Guard to track them in case their plan went south. Even if they were doing the Council's bidding, they knew all too well that the Guard took too many liberties during questioning. She rubbed her arm where the faint scar Adohan had given her when he was torturing her was located. She never wanted to have another reminder etched into her skin. Unfortunately, even with the advanced healing methods of the Royal system, some scars never fully heal.

She reviewed the flight plan and jump stations with Z once they were on the bridge. Z ensured her that avoiding the main jump stations was the best way to keep from tipping Apaleo off, in case he had any friends on the inside. Lexy wasn't so sure that man knew how to make friends let alone keep them, after pissing off the Council.

Once she confirmed everything, Lexy went to her room and showered before sliding into bed and falling into a dreamless sleep.

The following day she woke up before any of the others. She braided her hair and dressed in casual clothing. Today they were just going to watch Nora's daily schedule, so they had to blend in. She walked into the common room for some breakfast. Ali and Trent were already sitting next to each other, chatting and eating. Lexy's gut twisted. She quickly looked away and disappeared into the kitchen. After all, why should she care if they got along? Ali was her best friend, and Trent had quickly become one of her most trusted friends. If they got together, shouldn't she be glad for them?

She warmed a breakfast burrito and made a pot of coffee.

Trent walked up to the counter. "Mind if I get some of that coffee?"

"Sure," she replied, avoiding eye contact.

He grabbed two mugs, filling them both. In one, he added sugar and honey to the other. That was how Ali took her coffee. Her stomach did a flop. She shoved the burrito into her mouth, taking a bigger bite than she meant to. She turned away before Trent could see the pain in her eyes as they began watering. She always forgot to let food cool before taking a bite.

"Still hot?"

Damn, he noticed.

She nodded.

He chuckled. "Be careful. We need our Captain if this is going to work."

He picked up the mugs and took them back to the table. Lexy opened her mouth, inhaling and exhaling in an effort to cool the half-masticated food. Z walked in as she was finally able to swallow her food.

"Man, Lex, you have gotta stop burning your mouth." He grabbed a mug and filled it with coffee, "Let the damn thing cool. It says so on the package."

She groaned and followed him out of the kitchen. Ali patted the chair next to her. Lexy sat down, blowing on her still steaming food.

"I was just telling Trent about the history of Aria."

Lexy looked at Trent.

"And you're still awake?" Lexy teased.

Ali giggled. "You know I love history. Take Earth, for instance. Your people have encountered other beings since the Grays created you, but yet your government and religious systems still refuse to acknowledge us. I especially love the stories about a group that tries to keep these encounters secret."

Trent coughed into his coffee. "You guys know about the men in black?"

Ali handed him a napkin. "If that's what they are called, then yes. It's sad. I have seen so many civilizations refuse to believe that they are not alone because it doesn't fit their views. Even when a group of us land on their planet and say hello. That's what just happened near the Lyra constellation. A team went to make first contact, and the inhabitants attacked them. Now they're under a no visitation order until it's all sorted out."

Trent sipped his coffee. "I think for Earth, it's more of a we've-seen-the-way-society-handles-crisis-and-they're-not-ready-for-aliens kind of thing."

Lexy nodded in agreement.

Z took a seat next to Trent. "If only Earthlings knew how many nonEarthlings lived there."

Lexy finished her burrito and wiped her hands on her napkin.

"Okay, so back to the task at hand. Ali, how are we doing on the wiretapping?"

"I'm ready. All I have to do is lock Khunda's systems on the place of residence. Which I will do with a location tag Lo was working on. He assured me it works, it just hasn't gone through the CTA testing standards," she explained, taking her plate and mug to the dishwasher.

"Good," Lexy glanced around the common room. "Where is Marcus?"

They all shrugged.

Lexy sighed.

"I'll go get him. More than likely, he's primping."

She took the elevator to the guest quarters and knocked on his door. Jazz music met her ears. He always listened to it while he was getting ready for his day. Her thoughts floated back to the mornings she would wake up to him freshly showered and half covered. Often he would pull her off the bed to dance until they tumbled back into bed. Lexy's lips pulled at the corners at the thought of Marcus with just a towel on. She shook her head.

What the hell, Lex?

She knocked again. This time the door opened, and a shirtless Marcus smiled at her.

"I knew you remembered which room I preferred. How many times did you have to sneak down here before Z found out we were together?"

Lexy put her hands on her hips. "Whatever. I was just coming to get you. We're going to be docking soon, and I need to make sure you're not going to dress to impress. We're supposed to be undercover, remember?"

He leaned against the door frame. "I was thinking about going like this," he said, flexing his arm, "Maybe I could woo this Nora person, and she will just tell us where Apaleo is."

Lexy couldn't help but look him up and down. His tan skin was well-defined. She remembered how smooth it was and how the muscles underneath flexed when he held her. She took a step back without thinking about it. His face lit up. She knew she had given away her thoughts.

"Do you remember this song? We used to dance to it all the time. Dance with me," he commanded, extending his hand. She looked at it.

"Ah, we have shit to do, Marcus."

"Like what?" he grabbed her hand and pulled her into him. He led her in a slow, tight circle, "You used to love dancing with me. Your smile lit up the room, remember?"

Lexy smiled, remembering how happy she was when things were good between them. She tried not to look at him. Instead, she looked over his shoulder, but she could feel his heart pounding in his chest. His heat radiated, and somehow it made her body react without permission.

Geeze, it's hot in here.

"I remember. I still do. It was never the song that was the problem."

"You have to know how sorry I am about that. It was stupid, and I've regretted it every minute of every day since," he whispered into her ear, sending knee-weakening passion through her body.

Lexy let him turn her chin to face him, her heart felt like it would pound out of her chest as she looked into his blue eyes. There was always a weakness when it came to Marcus. She wanted to stay mad at him, but easier said than done. He hadn't shaved, and his hair was starting to darken his cheeks. Her face was so close to his. Without letting herself think about it, she raised to her toes, and her lips touched his, causing the spark to ignite into a full-on forest fire.

Marcus' hand wrapped behind her neck and pulled her into him further. She opened her mouth, her tongue searching for his. She pressed into him feeling his pulse pounding in his chest faster with each kiss. A moan came from somewhere deep within her.

Pulling away, she placed her finger on his lips.

"I loved you and you broke my heart." Her eyes raised to meet his, "There is no doubt the passion is still here, but without trust how can love grow?"

Marcus leaned his forehead against hers, "I know. I know I broke us and I will do everything I can to put the pieces back together. I'm asking you for a chance and if you say no then I will understand. We will finish this mission and I still stay as far away from you as you like, but," he took a deep breath, "If you let me, I will prove to you I've changed."

Tears filled Lexy's eyes. She leaned into his hand as he wiped them away as they fell down her cheeks.

"I will think about it," she whispered.

Marcus kissed her forehead.

"I promise I will respect your decision."

Lexy let him pull her into a deep hug. Her heart still ached for him. Love is confusing that way. After a moment she stepped away from his arms feeling cold and alone.

"We need to get to work. Meet us in the cargo bay."

Lexy turned and left without meeting his eyes. When it came to Marcus her restraint had always been nonexistent. It scared her how much she loved him. It took all of the strength she had at that moment not to turn back when she heard the door close behind her.

Chapter Seven

Aria was a lush planet with very few cities. Most of the tribes built their own capital where their government, markets, and training centers were run. Other than that, most of the inhabitants lived spread out across rolling green hills. The civilians too old or too young to serve the Royals ran farms and mills. Those with ailments often worked as shopkeepers.

Lexy stood just inside the capital city square of the Utu tribe, waiting for Trent to buy them snacks from a nearby food cart. Beings walked up and down the city streets, making no impact on the millions of thoughts running through Lexy's mind.

Just a few hours ago she and Marcus shared a kiss so passionate it was causing her to question everything. What did it mean? Did she still love him? Or did she just have zero self-control?

She slapped her forehead. *Stupid.*

"You okay?" Trent asked, handing her a napkin-wrapped sandwich.

She took it from him, hoping he couldn't see her cheeks turning red.

"Yeah, I'm fine. Just a bug or something."

Yep, it's something alright.

"Any updates?" he asked.

Lexy picked at the outer layer of her food. "No, they must still be on the train. This Nora lives just on the edge of the city. Why doesn't she just walk here? It's not that far."

Trent shrugged, taking a bite of his bread. "From what I could understand, that is fried bread with beans, cheese, and some vegetables on it," he said, pointing to Lexy's picked-at snack.

She took a bite, examining the ingredients stuffed inside.

"Not bad," she said.

"Okay guys, we just got off the train and we're headed toward the market," Ali's voice spoke through the ear comms.

Lexy looked up and down the street. The square was packed with beings buying, selling, and trading goods. Children weaved through the crowds with ease. Watching the scene reminded her of the farmer's market back home in Whitefish, Montana, where she met Trent for the first time. She had been working on her last book when Bones led him to her bench. Her chest ached for those days before the Royal mission messed up her plans.

"We're near their version of food trucks. I think the market is over there," she said, pointing across the center of the square.

Lexy took the last bite of her food before tossing the napkin into a bin. Trent followed her as they slipped into the flow of the crowd. Most of the planet's inhabitants were humanoid, but there was a small mix of other beings. They pushed past a small group of Grays haggling over the price of pastries. Lexy ducked when a nordic flailed his arms as he showed his disgust at the selection of grilled fish.

Once they reached the center of the square, Lexy climbed to the top of a wooden platform, most likely used for meetings and auctions. Marcus told them on the flight over that the Utu tribe was known for their livestock auctions. Currently, it was being used by several children acting out a battle. Lexy stopped to let a small girl, about six years old, pass her. *Children that young shouldn't know about war,* she thought. Shaking her head, she looked out at the streets lined with carts, each selling various goods and animals.

To the left, the street was lined with farmers and their produce. She squinted, sorting through the beings up and down the rows of stalls. Ali's blonde hair stood out, as she hurried after a woman with a bag slung over one shoulder. Marcus was just behind Ali, maneuvering her with his hand on her lower back. A flash of jealousy made Lexy's face warm. Seeing Marcus with any woman, even Ali, made all of the emotions of their breakup come flooding back.

"Everything okay, Lex?" Trent asked, coming to stand next to her.

She cleared her throat, shifting her eyes to follow Nora. "Yeah. I found them. They're right there near the cart with the chickens, at least they look like chickens."

Trent followed her gaze and led the way back down the stairs. Taking her hand he pulled her between stalls and around beings that stopped to talk. He was taller than her and could see over most of the crowd. The traffic thinned and Lexy caught sight of Nora once more. She watched as the woman manuvered through the streets with unwavering focus.

Lexy touched her ear. "You guys are heading toward a building with heavy security. Be careful."

She and Trent found a bench near the entrance, sitting so close to each other that they would seem like a young couple.

"Do you think he's in there?" Trent asked, setting his hand on her knee. This small action made her pulse quicken.

One good kiss and I can no longer control my hormones. What the hell, Lexy?

"No, those symbols above the door translate to a place for keeping. I think it's their version of a bank."

She placed her hand on his. The warmth he gave off calmed her reaction.

"Maybe she just has to pay her bills," he joked.

Lexy smiled. "Ali said she received a call before she left the house. She was getting a supply list. Who else would send her a grocery list?"

"I don't know, but Ali and Marcus are over there," Trent said, pointing down the street a few yards.

Lexy followed his gaze. Ali grabbed Marcus' hand and pulled him toward a nearby shop window, pointing toward a dress.

Nora passed them, hurrying up the stairs and into the building. They waited sitting close together on the bench for her to come back out. Lexy looked around as civilians past by. A small boy, holding his father's pinky, pointed to a woman waiting on the other side of the street for them. The boy let go of his father and rushed into the arms of the woman. His mother lifted him into a hug and kissed his cheeks. Lexy watched with a smile on her face. The scene reminded her of Adohan's words. She never thought about Apaleo having a family. Guilt filled her as she realized that she had been so consumed with her own life that she rarely thought about the beings that lived on planets like Aria. The scene in front of her gave her the feeling that people here were a lot like the ones on Earth.

Lexy shifted her weight.

"Is your butt going numb, too?" Trent asked with a chuckle.

"No, but I can't feel my legs anymore," she responded, not wanting to spill her thoughts to him.

Ali's voice rang in her ear.

"How much longer do you think I can stare in this window without someone thinking we're casing the joint?"

"Well, if you do decide to rob it, can you pick out something nice for my mom?" Z chimed in. He sounded bored, hanging back with the jump ship.

Lexy glanced back at the door. Nora walked out, her pace considerably faster than when she went in.

"It looks like we're going to get our exercise today. She's really huffing it," she noted, trying to stand as pins and needles shot down her legs. "She's clutching her bag. She must have picked up something."

Ali and Marcus began strolling back up the street, trying to look like they belonged.

"Trent and I are going to the next street over. Keep us posted."

She and Trent dodged between a couple of hover carts and down an alley to the next street. This one had shops lining the one-way road and was less crowded.

She and Trent walked a couple of blocks before turning into an alley that led them to the city's square. She took note of the statues of leaders killed in the war as they waited to cross the main road. Many of them looked too young to drink, let alone be war heros.

"Uh, guys I think she's on to us," Ali said, sounding nervous.

"Why do you say that?" Lexy questioned.

"Because she changed train cars once we took a seat. Should we follow?"

Lexy looked at Trent, and he took her hand, leading her across the square, toward the train station.

"No, stay where you are. Trent and I will try to get there."

They broke into a fast walk, weaving around beings. Once they reached the station, lights above the doors began to flash. They passed a car with Ali and Marcus sitting just inside the doors. Trent pulled her toward the next car, searching the windows. Nora stood near the first door. They walked one door down, taking a seat just close enough to see Nora looking around nervously, still gripping her bag tightly.

Just as the doors began to close, Nora stepped back out onto the platform and disappeared.

"Shit," Trent whispered.

"Ali, she just jumped ship," Lexy shifted in her seat trying to see where she had gone. The train jolted as it began to move.

"Ali, do you have a visual?" Lexy asked.

Trent pretended to stretch out his back, looking over his shoulder, "Damn, she's good."

"She's back here with us." Ali's winded voice came over the comm.

"Might need help." Marcus' responded, sounding hurried.

Trent stood looking toward the end of the car.

"There's an access door," he told Lexy.

They approached the door, trying not to draw attention from the people around them. Many of them had been trained as fighters and they didn't need that kind of complication right now. Lexy grabbed the handle, but the door was locked. She looked at Trent, who was digging around in his pocket. Whatever he grabbed, he leaned past her and touched it next to the lock. They heard a click. Lexy tried the door again. This time it opened.

"New tech?" she asked.

"Yeah, I nabbed it from the box Lo gave us." He shrugged.

"So, we aren't listening to the captain anymore?" she asked over her shoulder as they walked through the door into the next car.

Trent didn't respond as they walked into a stand-off between Ali and Nora. The rest of the car was empty of civilians.

Nora turned her head just enough to see them.

"Uh, guys. Are you okay?" Z had heard Marcus' last remark and must've gotten worried.

"Are you with her?" Nora asked, nodding toward Ali.

"She marked us," Ali groaned, "She walked into our car, yelled a word, and everyone else cleared out."

"Then she kicked our ass," Marcus finished from somewhere behind Ali.

Lexy raised her hands to show she didn't have a weapon. "We are with them, but we're not here to hurt you. We just want to ask-"

"I know why you're here and it won't work," She looked at Ali, "I can take you this time. Hand-to-hand combat isn't a strength for Guard members."

"Guys?" Z sounded nervous.

Trent stepped forward with his hands up.

"We're not Guard members. We work for the CTA. We worked with Apaleo."

Her eyes shot back at Trent at the mention of the CTA.

"I'm Captain Lexy Greggs. I was on that last mission with Apaleo. I'm the one he betrayed."

Nora's eyes widened in recognition, then squinted in anger.

"He had no choice. Apaleo would never have done that without being backed into a corner."

"Okay, you have five seconds before I come after you. 5... 4..." Z continued.

Ali touched her ear, "We are good for now, Z."

Lexy pulled up her sleeve to show the faint scar that Adohan had given her. "Yeah I thought so too, but I was the one he handed over to be tortured. So, sorry if I don't believe you."

Nora relaxed her stance a little.

"Why don't you go read the Guard's files? I already told them everything under truth serum."

Lexy dropped her hands.

"The Guard wouldn't use truth serum. That won't hold up in the courts, because the results can be swayed. The files say that you wouldn't talk to them."

Tears swelled in her eyes, "I wouldn't. That's why they held me down and gave me the shot."

Ali shook her head. "No, they wouldn't force someone to take a shot. It's against Royal law."

Nora's voice was shaking, "I'm telling the truth or are you too brainwashed?!" she yelled.

Trent sat down in a seat near her, but just out of reach. "I believe you."

Lexy stared at Trent. She couldn't believe what she was hearing. He motioned for her and Ali to sit down too. Lexy sat a few seats from Trent, looking for Marcus who was crouched on the other side of Ali with his weapon aimed at Nora. Ali must have stepped between them.

"Lexy and I are from Earth. We have a government that hides the truth from us too. I worked for them while we were at war, and some of the things you do during a war are things you'll never get out of your head."

Lexy never heard Trent talk about his time in the military. A tone in his voice told her that the memories were painful ones.

"This one time we were patrolling a village and a woman started shouting at us. We tried to calm her down, but she wouldn't. She shot my friend in the stomach. I returned fire, killing her. When we were sure she didn't have a bomb on her, we uncovered her face. She couldn't have been more than sixteen. I killed a child." His voice cracked. He cleared his throat and continued, "We found out that her brother was killed in a raid of their home. He was seven."

Lexy sat, mesmerized. His face was tight, and holding back emotions Lexy had never seen from him.

Trent cleared his throat and continued, "I wouldn't put it past any government, no matter how 'enlightened' they claim to be, to do what they feel is necessary to get their desired outcome."

Nora dropped to her knees sobbing. Ali rushed to her, wrapping her arms around her shoulders.

"Sounds like we've all been through some shit," Lexy said.

Marcus lowered his weapon, dropping to sit with his back to the wall. They sat in silence as Ali rocked Nora. The trauma of her encounter with the Guard seemed to all come flooding out. The tactics she described were banned by Royal law, but Lexy felt her trust in the Guard slip. She worked for them before the CTA and only knew a few members that would "bend" the rules to get what they wanted. Like a small crack in her faith, she began to question how far the Guard would go to protect the Royal system.

"I believe you," she whispered.

They all looked at her.

Lexy shrugged. "There are a lot of stars in the universe, and not every being is going to be a saint."

Nora nodded, wiping her tears. She grabbed her bag from under a chair. Lexy and Trent stood, hands on their weapons. Nora reached inside and pulled out a large wad of paper.

"I knew someone was following me, so I asked the bank for their trash to get you to show yourselves. It worked." She smiled at her own genius.

Trent looked at Lexy. Marcus stood, pointing his weapon at Nora, once more, before falling forward as the train slammed to a stop. They all fell, as warning lights flashed and emergency sirens began to wail.

Trent helped Lexy to her feet.

"WE HAVE COMPANY!" Z yelled.

Chapter Eight

The doors opened and they all ran out. Lexy grabbed Nora's arm before she could escape.

"Ali. Trent. Get Nora to the jump ship. Marcus, come with me, and let's see who's come to play." Lexy ordered.

They split up. The sound of gunfire caused Lexy's adrenaline to spike. She and Marcus began running toward the city center. They could see explosions and smoke filling the skyline. Screams rang out in the distance. They stopped a block from the center square pulling out their weapons.

"Who the hell would attack a Royal planet?" Marcus asked, taking in two of the bodies lying in the street.

"No one with half a brain," she responded, hoping the boy she watched earlier in the day was safe.

She grabbed Marcus' arm and pulled him into the final alley before the square. "You go left, I'll go right. Get eyes on the bad guys. Take out as many as you can. Don't be a cowboy. Just protect the civilians."

"Civilians." He scoffed, "These people are trained better than we are."

"Not the kids."

He rested his palm on her cheek, his eyes giving away his worry, before nodding. They left the safety of the alley and walked into the fight, guns pointed. Around the square, small skirmishes were raging. Lexy looked around, trying to distinguish who was a civilian and who was an enemy. Just ahead of her, a woman held off two men near the raised platform where children had been playing just an hour before. The woman held a knife, slicing at one of the attackers. Lexy took a stance, firing at the second man's leg and missing as he moved to strike the woman. His focus shifted to Lexy who closed in the space between them. She took another shot, knowing that the burst of energy would be smaller than the first, one of the fallbacks to an energy pulse weapon. The shot hit the man's shoulder, causing him to stumble back a couple of steps. Now that she was close enough, she raised her foot, kicking him in the gut and sending him backward into a stack of crates.

Lexy turned to see the woman pinned to the platform by the other attacker. Lexy holstered her weapon, picking up a metal pole lying near the stage. Before she could use it, the first man regained his footing and tackled Lexy to the ground. The air was forced from her lungs as the man's weight pressed down on her. Gripping the pole at both ends she forced it up and into her attacker's neck. The man gurgled as the pole cut off his oxygen. A rustling sound under the platform caught her attention; turning her head, she saw a small group of young children huddled together, hiding.

Lexy pushed the pole to her left, forcing most of the man's weight off of her. Her free leg found his groin, and the attacker rolled over in pain. Lexy jumped to her feet, raising the pole above her head before bringing it down on the head of the man choking the Utu woman. He slumped forward and fell to the ground. The woman rolled to the ground after him, coughing and gasping for air. Lexy pulled her weapon from its holster, shooting both attackers before turning her attention to the still-coughing woman.

"Are you okay?"

Lexy crouched down, and the dark-haired woman nodded.

"Good. Is there somewhere safe you can take these kids?" she asked, pointing to the children.

The woman looked around at the buildings lining the square. She sat back and choked out her reply, "Yes. The red building there has a safe room."

Lexy glanced at her gun's power-level light. It was at half-strength. She handed the woman the gun.

"Get them there and keep them safe. And don't make me regret giving you my gun."

The woman made eye contact with her. "I am of the warrior planet. I will protect my own. You should worry about your own ass," she responded, pushing the gun back at Lexy.

Hands raised Lexy replied, "No. I would rather it protect them." Lexy glanced toward the children.

The woman nodded and motioned to the children to follow her. Lexy kept watch as they crossed the street and slid through the door of the red building. Once they were inside, Lexy grabbed the pole again, looking around the square.

"I am of Earth and I do stupid shit, like give my only gun away. Crap." Lexy mumbled, knowing she would do it again in a heartbeat.

She moved to hide behind a merchant's deserted tent. This one sold small wooden toys, all of which looked to be handmade. She peeked at the display on the table.

Hey, these could help.

She thought, grabbing a couple of solid wooden balls and putting them in her pocket. The sound of a low-flying ship caused her hand to freeze over the second ball. The ground shook as explosions took out the platform in the square's center. Debris rained down on the table as she slid under it for protection. The crunch of boots running toward her hiding place forced her to hold her breath. She didn't know who they belonged to, they could be Guard members or more attackers. Two beings in similar suits as the men she fought jogged by her. They stood near the platform's remains. She could make out some of what they were saying.

"One of the shuttles saw two women shoot our men... They ran into that building..."

Oh, hell no.

Lexy emerged from under the table, grabbing the ball from her pocket. Debris crunching under her feet made the attackers turn to face her. She tossed the ball into the air and struck it with the pole. It connected with the woman's nose, and blood splattered the face of the blue-skinned man next to her. He closed the gap between them with perfect timing so Lexy could swing the pole back and hit the man's ribs. He fell forward, calling out in pain. She shifted out of his way as a laser grazed her shoulder. She dropped to a crouch, turning in the direction of the shot. A large man with scars across his face stood too close for Lexy's comfort. His weapon raised and pointed at her. She glanced to the left and right, nowhere to hide. Then, dropping the pole, she raised her hands and stood.

"You look too clean to be from this shit hole," he growled.

Lexy glanced over her shoulder as the two injured attackers stood, pointing their weapons at her.

"Speaking of shit hole, have you looked in a mirror lately?" she asked.

Someone kicked her knee out, forcing her to drop to the ground.

"Not so cocky now, are you?" the female asked Lexy through the sleeve she was using to stop the bleeding.

The man with the scars came to stand in front of her. He pushed the pole out of her reach with his boot. The sound of it bouncing away was drowned out by the ship overhead making another pass, shooting at some unknown target. The man holstered his weapon and pulled her up by her hair. He looked her over, his face twisting with disgust.

"Let's see who you are." He touched his ear. "Commander we have someone of interest, and we're bringing her to you."

Turning, he pulled Lexy down the aisle, toward an open space filled with beings in similar clothing. Fear settled in her chest, its grip tightening, causing her breathing to quicken. She started slapping at the man's grip.

"Let me...go!" she yelled.

He laughed in response.

Shit. Shit. Shit.

She couldn't think. It was as if the fear had turned off her logic. Darkness began to creep into her periphery. She clawed at his arm and punched at his side. He laughed louder. She tried kicking at him but stumbled and fell to her knees. The man dragged her to the center of a small crowd. Several other beings, dressed in casual clothes, were lined up to her left. Civilians. All of them were on their knees, waiting. Lexy didn't want to know why they were waiting.

"This one may be of value," the man with the scars called to a woman holding a scanner up to a tan young man at the end of the line. He looked to be in his early twenties.

"Be right there," the woman responded.

That voice. Lexy shifted to sit up just to be kicked back down. From where she was lying Lexy watched the woman's figure, as she pulled her weapon and shot the being she had just scanned. Reholstering the gun, she began walking toward Lexy and her scarred captor. Lexy's heart jumped into her throat.

That can't be. This isn't right.

Words wouldn't come to Lexy. She was still trying to figure out how it was possible. Then, as the woman approached, a smile of recognition spread across her face.

Someone pulled Lexy up by the back of her shirt. Her eyes widened as the tattoo on the woman's neck confirmed her fears. A black, nine-pointed star peeked from under the woman's collar. The symbol was a common tattoo Royal Guard members would get.

"Nala. What are you doing? You're a member of the Guard. Why are you attacking a Royal planet?" Lexy demanded.

Nala looked at the civilians in the line. She nodded to the man who had a hold of Lexy. He and several others began leading the civilians away at gunpoint. Lexy watched in fear for their lives. Whatever was happening, she had a feeling Royal laws no longer applied.

Nala looked Lexy up and down. "Captain Lexy Greggs. Funny meeting you here."

"Not that funny. I'm on Council business, and I demand an answer. Why have you attacked a planet under Royal protection?" Lexy demanded, standing taller.

Nala laughed.

"I heard. Are you an errand girl now? You always were too big for your shiny ship."

Lexy stepped forward, bringing herself nose-to-nose with Nala.

"I'm only going to ask you one more time. Why have you attacked these people?" she demanded, her voice tight with anger.

The woman's smile reminded Lexy of the last encounter they had. One year into Lexy's time with the Guard, she worked with Nala on a mission. The woman was cruel on the best of days. After Lexy reported her to their superiors for immoral tactics, the woman disappeared. Lexy always figured she was jailed or banished to a primitive planet for her actions.

"I don't answer to you, remember? You're all high and mighty now, working for the CTA. It must be nice to have connections. As for the rest of us, we actually have to work for a living," Nala spat at her. "And besides, I'm a part of the rebellion now. Can't you tell by my tatty clothes and riff-raff crew?"

Lexy cocked her head, confused by Nala's confession. But before she could respond, Marcus stepped around a stack of crates, a gun pressed into his back by a large man with a swollen eye.

Nala started laughing. "Oh, this is good. Two CTA captains for the price of one."

Marcus looked at Lexy questioningly.

"Marcus, this is crazy, murderous bitch. Crazy, murderous bitch this is Marcus."

Nala swung the scanner across Lexy's face, causing stars to burst through her vision and her ears to ring. Marcus caught Lexy before she hit the ground. He yelled at Nala, but his voice sounded as if they were underwater. She blinked several times until she could see straight again. Marcus' face was looking at hers, checking her injury.

"You okay?" he asked.

She nodded, turning to look at their captor. Nala's fingertips were touching in front of her face.

"Oh, I see now. You two are in love?"

The few members of her crew that were left, laughed.

"Fuck off." Lexy spat.

"That's not very nice, Captain Greggs. Someone should teach you manners." Nala pulled her weapon from its holster. "Now, which one gets to watch the other die?"

Marcus pushed Lexy behind him as Nala pulled the trigger. The impact sent his blood in every direction. Marcus' weight slammed into Lexy. She slid to the ground, supporting him from behind. Setting him down, she ripped his shirt open in search of the wound. Blood oozed from a hole in his shoulder. Oozing was better than squirting, but not much. She took off her jacket, pressing it into his wound.

"Shit, that hurts," he said, reaching to feel the hole.

Lexy slapped his hand away, "Yeah, gunshots do." Lexy examined the injury, and from what she could see, this looked like a wound from a projectile, not a laser or energy pulse.

She faced Nala. "Using primitive weapons now? That seems a step down for even a lowlife like you."

Nala raised the gun again, aiming for Lexy, who closed her eyes as the shot echoed off the buildings. No pain ripped through her tense body. Opening her eyes, she found Nala pinned to the ground by a large man, who had taken her gun and begun firing at the crew members. Lexy dropped her body over Marcus'. His arms tightened around her as he rolled, so his body was protecting her. He cried out in pain. When the shots stopped, Lexy lifted her head to see the damage. The man was facing away from them. Just beyond him, Nala and two crew members were running away. She sat up, looking for a weapon of her own. Marcus' grunts as he began to sit up brought the man's attention back to them.

Her hand reaching for an abandoned gun, Lexy froze as the man turned to face her. "Apaleo."

Chapter Nine

Apaleo stood to face her. Lexy's hand found a gun as Marcus pulled himself up to his knees, cursing. Another round of attacks from the ship rang out, the smoke rising a couple of blocks south of their location.

Lexy helped Marcus to his feet, keeping the gun ready, hoping he didn't attack. The man was one the best fighters she had ever seen, and she was starting to get the feeling that his training went way beyond the basic Guard training she had received.

His pants were dirty, as if he had spent some time camping in the wilderness. The short hair that outlined his jaw and throat confirmed that he hadn't been hiding in comfort.

Good.

Apaleo's eyes shifted and narrowed over Lexy's head. "Took him long enough," he grumbled.

She heard the hum of a small ship approaching. Glancing over her shoulder, she watched the jump ship land a few yards away, kicking up dust and dirt.

"There you are, Lex," Z's voice rang in her ear. "We've been looking all over for you two. Did you notice someone is attacking? And you thought it was a good idea to go running off with Captain Fancy Pants. What the-"

"Not a good time, Z," Marcus scolded.

Lexy looked back at Apaleo as he tucked the gun into his waistband, shifting his weight to step forward, "Where the hell do you think you're going?" she asked.

Apaleo a step toward the jump ship. Lexy pointed her gun at his chest, stopping him in his tracks. The back of the jump ship opened, and Trent jogged to them with his weapon drawn. Recognition crossed his face as he came to stand next to Lexy.

"Marcus get on board," Lexy ordered.

He looked at Lexy, and then back at Apaleo before turning toward the ship, cursing with every step. She listened for his boots to connect with the metal ramp.

"Want me to shoot him?" Trent asked, aiming.

"No. We need him alive."

Apaleo slowly raised his hands. "I saved your life."

Lexy's lip raised in disgust. "Look around. You saved me from the same people you betrayed me for. Get onboard," she commanded, sounding stronger than she felt.

Seeing Apaleo had her insides twisting. She wanted to cry, yell, and strangle him all at the same time. This was the man she trusted with her life and the lives of her crew on more than one mission. He betrayed them, handing over King Edward and Lexy to that scum Adohan. Now, with any luck, they would be locked up in the same prison, maybe even cellmates. The same slivers of fear that hid behind Adohan's eyes would be hiding behind Apaleo's for the rest of his life.

Keeping his hands raised, he started to pass her when shots rang out. Apaleo grabbed Lexy and Trent by the arms, pulling them to the ground. She tried to roll away from him, but he held her in place. The smell of dirt, sweat, and blood flooded her nose as she fought against his grip. Trent and Apaleo shifted so they could raise their weapons toward the gunfire. As both men began shooting at their targets, Apaleo's free arm pushed Lexy into Trent's shoulder.

"Get her to the jump ship," he instructed his voice a low growl.

Trent nodded, grabbing Lexy around the waist. She let him lead her onto the ramp and into the ship's safety. Looking back, she saw Apaleo take out two of the rebels before turning and sprinting on board next to her.

The ramp closed, and Z maneuvered them into the air. The ship pitched as they turned and gained speed. Ali tended to Marcus' injury while strapping him to a chair on the far wall, Apaleo hugged and talked in low voices with Nora. Trent pointed his weapon at Apaleo's head.

"Um, hey guys, I could use some help up here," Z called back to them.

Lexy walked to Apaleo. "Give me the gun," she demanded. Apaleo hesitated. "or I will let him shoot you," she said, nodding at Trent.

Trent winked at him. With reluctance, Apaleo handed over the gun. Lexy checked the ammo. Only three bullets left. Apaleo was spot on with a gun, but that didn't matter, he could take them all out without one shot fired.

Why did he save us? Why didn't he let Nala kill me?

Lexy didn't have time for questions. They needed to stop the attacks, and she knew that Apaleo would be on board for that.

"You and Trent on the gunners. Ali, keep Marcus alive. Z, we are going after that ship," she called out, sliding her gun into her empty holster and handing the extra one to Trent. She led Trent and Apaleo to the front of the craft, where Z was in his chair frantically typing on the console.

Lexy jumped into her seat, pulling up the ship's exterior cameras, "What's happening, Z?"

"Trying to get eyes on-" laser blasts hit the ship just outside the window cutting him off and causing them to jolt to the left, "Yeah, that."

Lexy stretched her neck, looking at the scorch marks on the ship's nose. She started pulling on her harness.

"Strap in, everyone," she yelled.

Behind her, Trent and Apaleo slipped into two chairs controlling the small ship's minimal weapons. Maybe they should have upgraded the jump ship before leaving Alpha Orion.

"Ready to kick some ass, Lex," Z chuckled.

"Charge all weapons. Let's go, Z."

Z pushed the accelerator forward, and they took off after the rebel ship. He maneuvered them through the tall buildings, keeping the attacking ship within view.

"Z, you're going to have to get closer. Our guns won't reach that far."

Lexy was doing all she could to reroute as much power as possible to the engines. The rebel ship was much faster. There must be some fancy power systems aboard to keep a junker like that from blowing up, she thought. They jolted to the left.

"Oops, clipped a building," Z explained, shrugging.

"Could we not hit anything? Unless it's the ship that's shooting at us."

Lexy glanced back at Trent and Apaleo, hologram screens controlled by their neural impulses, floated in front of their eyes. Lights flashed across their screens as they tried locking onto the ship before firing. Lexy turned back to the window, but there was no ship in sight.

"Where -"

"Wait for it," Z warned.

The ship rounded a building coming straight for them.

Apaleo and Trent began firing. The rebel ship pulled up hard.

"Where do you think you're going?" Z questioned, pulling them into a vertical climb.

Both ships sped toward space. The jump ship began to shake. If this had been the first time they'd had a fast ascent, Lexy may have been worried. But it wasn't. She had complete confidence in her pilot.

Lexy looked at Z and then back at the rebel ship.

Why would rebels attack a planet they say they are fighting for? And do they have engines that can outrun my jump ship?

By the time they broke through the atmosphere, the rebel ship was out of weapons range. A burst of blue and white light shot out of the rebel ship's thrusters, and the ship gained more speed than the jump ship could.

"Damnit," Z yelled, slamming his hand on the console.

Lexy slumped back into her chair. "Crap."

Apaleo and Trent disengaged from the weapons systems, holo screens fading from sight.

"They moved fast for a rusty old ship," Trent said, rubbing his eyes with the palm on his hands, "There is no way that thrust system came standard."

"Yeah, and those don't come cheap. How could the rebels afford that?" Z asked.

Lexy released her buckle, "I don't understand. What kind of ship do you think that was, Z?"

Z unbuckled his harness, "That looked like an old-school BX22. Those things can't go that fast."

"I didn't think so either," Lexy mumbled.

Ali walked up to the console and pushed a few buttons.

"Lucky for you, I updated all of your exterior cameras before we left and now we have high-quality pictures of the ship and its markings."

Images of the rebel ship popped into view on the main screen, as the real thing flew further out of sight. Lexy jumped up, kissing Ali on the cheek.

"You are amazing! This is awesome. Khunda, can you run these images through the Royal registration database and see if you can find a match."

"Yes, Captain."

Lexy slid her arms out of her harness, "Get us back to Khunda, Z."

"Yes, ma'am," Z responded, saluting her. "But first…"

Z swung around to face Apaleo, shooting him in the neck with a dart. Then, he shifted his aim and shot Nora as she rushed to catch Apaleo as he fell. They both hit the ground hard, and Z blew on the gun barrel.

"You brought a tranquilizer gun?" Lexy asked, unable to hide her shock.

Trent kicked Apaleo with his toe. "Looks like it." He chuckled, stepping over Apaleo's unconscious body to give Z a high five.

Lexy shook her head. "So, what happened to energy pulse guns only? I would lock you up for insubordination, except I need you to fly the ship."

Z looked from the two bodies on the floor to Lexy. "Oh, you're just mad that you didn't get to shoot them."

Lexy shrugged. "Maybe. I'm going to check on Marcus. Get us to Khunda, Z."

Ali bent down to check Nora's pulse. "What should we do with them?"

Lexy waved her hand over her shoulder. "Just leave them there."

Z steered the small ship back to Khunda. Lexy sat next to Marcus until they landed in the cargo bay. Khunda sat hidden on the dark side of one of Aria's three moons.

Once the jump ship's door opened, Ali and Lexy helped Marcus into Khunda's small medical room in the back of the cargo bay. Trent carried Nora and Apaleo toward the holding cells tucked in the opposite corner of the bay. Z took off for the bridge mumbling something about wanting to ask around about the rebel ship. Ali had more experience with patching up wounds, so Lexy left her to fix up Marcus after squeezing his hand. Standing in front of the jump ship, she looked around the cargo bay reviewing the attack on Aria. Trent sat on a stool outside the holding cells holding a laser pulse pistol that would burn a hole through its target. Lexy knew he would use it if he had to.

Releasing a long sigh, she ran her hand along the scorch mark the rebels left on the jump ship. That was going to be a pain to buff out.

"Lex!" Z yelled before the elevator door was fully open.

Now what?

Z jumped over the railing, a ComBoard in his hand.

"You are going to want to see this," he said, pushing the board into her palm.

Lexy rotated the board and waited the split second it took for the language to change to English. She began reading:

Breaking News Bulletin*. There has been an airborne attack on the Utu tribe of the planet Aria. Several were killed, and hundreds were injured. The details of the unprovoked attack are unknown. Royal Guard members are on the scene, and all surveillance videos were taken into Royal Guard custody. Witnesses have identified one of the attacking ships and its crew as members of the violent group who claim to be rebels of the*

Royal system. The second ship has been identified as the Class A transport ship Khunda and her crew Captain Alexendra Greggs of Earth, Captain Marcus Curran of Beta Leo, Zephla of Alpha Orion, Aliana of Cassiopeia Prime, and Security officer Brandon Trent of Earth. We have reached out to Director Ameran of the Central Transport Agency for a comment on one of the agency's ships attacking a Royal planet. She refuses to comment.

The Khunda and her crew have been under review for harboring and aiding a member of the violent rebel group while transporting the current King of Alpha Virgo to his coronation just a few weeks ago.

We will update this story as we get more information.

Lexy's jaw dropped.

Z nodded, "Yeah, that's what I thought, too."

Lexy reread the section tying them to the attack.

"We didn't … how are we… YOU HAVE GOT TO BE FUCKING KIDDING ME?!" she burst out.

Lexy glanced around. Through the glass wall, she watched Marcus push himself up to sit as Ali argued with him, suture supplies still in her hands. He looked at her questioningly. Lexy shook her head and glanced back at the board.

Tears of anger filled her eyes. At that moment, the pieces all snapped into place. This was their plan. This is why the Counsel sent them to catch Apaleo. She let her gaze slide over the new tech still spread over the table in the bay's repair room. How did she not see this coming? She knew members of the Counsel wanted just one more reason to push the vote through on the Grey planets. Here was their motive. She and Trent were from Earth, and if anyone dug deep enough, they would find that it was the home planet of Marcus's mother. Three members of the CTA from Earth going full-on rebel would be enough to get any Counsel member to vote. It would put Earth in their crosshairs.

There had to be a way to flip the narrative. A way to get the Counsel to listen to them. Trent moved to stand in the doorway between the cells and the cargo bay. She handed Z his ComBoard back.

"Lex?"

"Z, get back to the bridge. We need to go silent. I don't want anyone knowing where we are until we are ready to be found," she commanded over her shoulder as she made her way to the table covered in the tech, "Pull our CTA beacon and find a cave to hide in."

Z stood at the door, as she grabbed what she needed.

It's time someone told the truth.

"What are you going to do, Lex?" he asked, concern in his voice.

"Lex, what's going on?" Marcus asked, holding his shoulder as he slumped in the doorway of the medical room.

"Ali, patch him up," she snapped, loading the dart gun with the green dart. "Z, I gave you orders."

Lexy moved past Trent. "Lock me in and don't let any of the others in. Got it?" she demanded.

He shifted his footing so that he was in the room with her. Trent pushed buttons on the control panel, and the clear door slid closed with a click letting her know it couldn't be opened from the outside.

"This is your fight. I'm just here to put the dog down if it comes to it," he told her, checking that his weapon was fully charged.

Z, Marcus, and Ali were at the sealed door yelling. The space was soundproof, so Trent and Lexy couldn't hear what they were saying. Taking a deep breath, she moved to stand in front of the cell that held Apaleo.

Trent stood at the control panel, "You sure about this, Lexy?"

She looked over Apaleo's unconscious body. He was taller, stronger, and more skilled than her. This was definitely a bad idea, but it was her only one. She nodded without looking at Trent. She knew if there were any hint of worry in his eyes, she would lose her nerve.

The door to the cell slid open, but before Lexy could take the shot, Apaleo jumped up, grabbed her by the shirt, pulling her into the cell. The dart gun fired as her elbow snapped up to connect with Apaleo's jaw. He slammed her back into the cell wall.

"Going to shoot a sleeping target?" he asked, pulling the gun from her hand.

"But you weren't really sleeping, were you?" she choked, his forearm pressed into her throat.

"No. They start us on small doses of tranquilizer drugs in training. That way, we have immunity."

"That sounds like a wonderful memory. What else did they do? Water board you if you got a bad grade, or did they just kick you in the nuts when you stepped out of line?" Lexy asked.

"Do you care what they did to us?" he spat at her.

"No, just making conversation."

Lexy swung her leg up to hook her knee around the opposite side of his neck. She arched her back. Apaleo lost his grip on her, and she fell to the floor. Rolling onto her back, she kept him in sight as she found her footing.

"Who taught you that move?" he asked, glancing at Trent. "No. Not him. Your military doesn't rely on hand-to-hand, do they? Maybe he learned it in the desert somewhere." Apaleo's eyes never left Trent as he spoke.

Lexy took the opportunity and, stepping forward, grabbed the back of his neck before pulling his head down into her knee. Apaleo grabbed her knee before it made contact. He lifted it, causing her to stagger into the doorway. Stumbling backward his eyes filled with shock. He reached to touch the back of his neck, where a silver disc the size of a quarter was attached to his skin.

"Dammit!" he roared.

Lexy stepped out of the cell, motioning to Trent once she crossed the threshold. He pressed a key on the panel, and Apaleo's door closed again.

"You okay, Lexy?" Trent asked.

Lexy rubbed her shoulder where she had landed on the floor. "Yeah, I'm good."

He glanced behind him, "What do you want me to do about them?" he asked, nodding at the rest of her crew glaring at her through the glass door.

"Open it."

He pressed the button, and the door slid open. All three of them stayed silent, waiting for her explanation.

"Khunda, open communications between us and confinement cell one."

"Yes, Captain. Communication is open."

Lexy shifted her weight. "I wouldn't play with that too much if I were you," she warned Apaleo. She had no idea what the disc would do if tampered with once it connected with a person's neuropathways. The device was still new, and Lexy had no clue if it had ever been tested successfully, but she was desperate.

The man rubbed at his dark skin, "What did you attach to my neck?"

Lexy smiled at him, "I think it's time you and I have an honest chat."

Chapter Ten

Lexy looked at Z, "We really need to go silent before the Guard starts looking for us."

Z glanced at Trent and then back to Lexy, "Fine. Khunda, record everything that happens while I'm not here."

"Yes, Zephla." This ship's polite tone responded, not fitting the tension among the group.

Lexy watched as Z headed for the elevator, taking all four stairs in one stretch. She hated not having him nearby. Of everyone aboard Khunda, he knew her the best. But if the Guard found them before they could find something to get the Counsel to listen, then they would never get a chance to prove their innocence. She refocused on Apaleo.

"So, why would you attack *your* people, the rebels, and save us, the ones you betrayed?"

Apaleo dropped his head, "Those were not rebels."

"Yes, they were. We have a video of the ship."

Ali walked to the cell door holding a comboard. She held it up for him to see. Apaleo shifted forward to watch the images. He shook his head, "That can't be. We would never attack our own. Can I see it closer?"

Lexy nodded at Ali, who used her hand to zoom in on a still of the rebel ship.

"That's not one of our ships."

Lexy snorted, "Of course, you'd say that. Maybe that truth disc thingy isn't working."

"No, really, Captain," he said, pointing to the images, "We don't have any ships with an after-market gold series thrust system, and we wouldn't display our tags on our ships. That would be a giveaway every time we passed by a guard station or ship." He rubbed the small silver device on his neck, "And this damn thing is working, because I can't even think up a lie. It's as if my brain no longer works that way."

He was right about the ship, that would be stupid.

Why would Nala claim to be with the rebels if she wasn't?

Trent stepped forward.

"Why would someone want to impersonate a rebel ship if it was that easy to get caught? Or better yet, how *didn't* they get caught?"

Ali left the room as Apaleo came to stand.

"I can't answer the how but I can answer the why and the who. The why is to commit atrocities while those who rebel get the blame. As for the who, the Royals have a million reasons to have an undercover crew."

Ali shook her head.

"No, the Royals support the effort to fight beings who go from planet to planet terrorizing peaceful citizens."

Apaleo looked at her.

"We were once peaceful beings as well, and then the Royals began overstepping their powers. And can you think of a better way to build support than to have control over attacks? As the Earth saying goes, kill one bird with two stones?"

Marcus snorted. "It's two birds with one stone, dumbass."

Lexy cocked her head, amazed that Apaleo remembered the analogy she used on their first mission together years ago. Since then, Apaleo severed as her head of security on more assignments than she could count. She had trusted him.

Lexy shook the thought from her head.

"If it was a team of Royal black ops, why wouldn't the rebels have called them out on it yet?"

Apaleo smirked. "They have. It just didn't make the news feed."

Lexy pinched the bridge of her nose. "Is that why you joined the rebels? Because the Royals were censoring the news?"

"No. I joined because I watched for years as the Royals and the Council pushed the enlightened planets around. That was the first mark against them," Apaleo grunted as he opened and closed his fists.

"And the second was?" Lexy waved her hand to get him to go on.

Apaleo glanced at Nora, who lay unconscious in the cell next to his, "I saw firsthand what they are capable of. I was in the Guard before the CTA. Royal security, to be specific."

Lexy's eyebrow rose. Royal security only chose the best of the best. Being security for a Royal was a coveted job among the Warrior tribes. Lexy crossed her arms, wondering what pushed him over the edge, what did he know that made him leave the Guard.

"You said you saw what they were capable of, what does that entail?" Trent asked.

Apaleo sat back against the metal wall, bringing his knees up to rest his forearms. He sighed as if choosing his words wisely.

"I was the prime protector for a queen on an alpha planet."

Lexy's eyebrows raised as she looked at Marcus and Ali for their reaction, which told her that this was news to them, too.

Why was that NOT in his files?

Apaleo continued, "At first, it was what you would expect. Following her around, observing but never reacting. I was to blend in wherever we went. Be unnoticed but always ready to protect," he sighed, the memories floating behind his eyes. "Then, one night, the queen called me to her chambers and dismissed her night guards. I thought I had done something wrong. That night I was cornered into fulfilling her," he paused, choosing his words carefully, "specific needs. If I tried to refuse after that first night, she would threaten to say that I raped her. There was no way out. She had her spies find Nora, and she would control me with threats. I did what I had to. I did it to keep her safe," He explained, looking at Nora's unconscious body.

Lexy shifted her weight, the adrenalin had run its course, leaving her drained. Looking at Apaleo's face, she realized the man was holding back emotions she had never seen from him. For so long, she questioned if he even had them. They worked together for years, while he held so many painful memories. Her eyes dropped to the floor, she couldn't meet his eyes while guilt filled her.

Trent was the first to break the silence. "How did you leave?"

Apaleo looked at Trent, "I met Ameran after a ball for the queen one night. She walked in into what she thought was an empty hall. Except, I was there with a gun to my head. After talking me out of putting a bullet through my brain, she offered me a job. Ameran knows far more about the Royals than she lets on." His eyes landed on Lexy as he finished the last sentence.

This small detail told Lexy know that he knew more about Ameran than she did, and it annoyed her. Lexy rubbed her hands together, she was beginning to see how using the truth disc could have been a bad idea.

She wanted to hate him, to keep him the bad guy. One bad guy would be easier to deal with than an entire government.

"If you owe Ameran your life, then why would you betray her and us? I thought the warriors had a code of honor." Lexy asked, a small squeak giving away her conflicting emotions.

Apaleo looked at Nora his eyebrows pinched together. Letting out a sigh, he turned his focus to the ceiling.

"Because of the Ancient blood theory."

He said the phrase in such a matter-of-fact tone that Lexy thought she had misheard him. She glanced at the others.

"Does anyone know what he is talking about?"

Marcus nodded.

"I've heard about it. Mostly through drunks in bars, but they all say it used to be in their school history feeds before it was cut out," he explained, sitting on a crate, gripping the bandage covering his wound. "The theory is that after the ancients left this side of the galaxy and the Royals took over ruling the enlightened, the ancients left a line of their genetics behind. All the geneticists claim if there was any DNA left behind, they would have found it by now. Some think that those with the ancient DNA were meant to rule after they left. "

Apaleo scoffed.

Lexy clenched her teeth. "You betrayed the CTA and Ameran for a conspiracy theory?"

Turning his back on her was one thing, but Ameran hired him when no one else would hire a warrior outside of the Royal security and the Guard. He got his dream job thanks to Ameran. He owed her everything.

"It's not a conspiracy theory. I found the geneticist who discovered the gene."

Lexy's mouth dropped open.

That can't be right.

"If the gene was found, why haven't we heard about it? These scientists have to use a lab, and all the Royal labs have open files."

"You never heard of it because a lab owned by the Royals found it. When they got the report, they put the geneticist into hiding. They knew that if it got out to the public, their rule over the enlightened planets would be threatened. I would go out searching for the geneticist between assignments. It took me years to find out where they hid her."

"I don't suppose you're willing to share that information with us?" Trent asked.

"Why do you think I saved you from those rebel imposters?"

Lexy's eyes widened as she clinched her fists. "Oh, *that's* why? Did it have nothing to do with the guilt of leaving me to be tortured to death? Or that you gave up King Edward to be decapitated on a live feed?"

Apaleo let out a low chuckle. "I thought you despised that spoiled brat."

"Just because I don't like someone doesn't mean they should die," Lexy snapped.

Apaleo moved to stand. "You would if you knew what the Royals had done."

Lexy shifted nervously, she didn't like his big movements, even if he was locked in a cell.

"And I was sorry that you were involved. I respected what your parents did –"

Anger filled Lexy, "Oh, No! You *do not* get to mention my parents."

He raised his hands in surrender.

Lexy pushed air out of her nose, stilling her shaky breath, before continuing.

"You mentioned what the Royals had done. How about you fill us in on that?" she asked, raising an eyebrow.

Shaking his head, he looked at Nora. "Maybe another time, Captain."

"Stop calling me that! I am no longer your Captain. You are my prisoner, and you'll pay for your crimes."

Crossing his arms, Apaleo leaned against the transparent wall. "Do you think the Counsel will change their story about you attacking Aria? They would never want to look weak, no matter who they have to kill to keep it a secret. No, the only option you have is to prove the existence of an Ancient bloodline and use the information as a bargaining tool."

"What makes you so sure the Royals will spare our lives?" Trent asked.

"I can't promise you they will, but it seems to be the only option you have."

Nora moaned and rolled onto her side. Apaleo squatted down and watched as she slowly sat up. She looked around, taking in her surroundings. Her mouth began moving, but the walls were soundproof.

"Khunda, turn off comms to holding cell one."

"Yes, Captain. Communication off."

"Good, now allow comms between the holding cells and record all of it."

Apaleo and Nora's mouths were moving, but they couldn't be heard. Lexy led Trent out of the room. She nodded to Trent, who entered a code to lock the doors behind them.

Trent, Ali, and Marcus looked at Lexy expectantly. Then, before she could answer, Z jogged out of the elevator doors. "What did I miss?"

Ali rested her hands on her hips. "Apaleo betrayed you guys for the location of a geneticist that, he says, discovered the Ancient bloodline."

Z took a moment to process the information. "Well, son-of-a-bitch, I always wondered if the stories were true."

Lexy looked at Marcus, who was still holding his gunshot wound. "Ali, please take Marcus back to medical and patch him up."

Marcus shifted out of Ali's reach. "Not until I know what you're planning, Lex."

"What makes you think I'm planning something?" she asked, chewing on her bottom lip.

"Because I know you. Your gears are turning, and chewing on your lip means you're torn on what to do."

"He's not wrong," Z agreed.

Lexy huffed and turned toward the jump ship. She felt years of loyalty to the Guard, the Council, and the Royals fall away. They had betrayed her just as Apaleo had. She and the crew were now marked as criminals. To her annoyance, Apaleo was right. They would never admit they were wrong in naming the crew of Khunda as terrorists. That would be a sign of weakness, and worse, it would cause people to question the actions of the Council and the Royal leaders. Questions are dangerous to those who want to stay in power. Lexy ran her hand along the scorch march on the jump ship's hull.

She jumped as Trent rested his hand on her shoulder. "Lexy, what's the plan?"

Only a small moment had passed, but the flood of thoughts in her head made her feel as if she was waking up from a long sleep.

She looked at Ali and Marcus. "Please, go to the med room and fix that wound. You're bleeding on my floors. Trent, brief me on all the weapons onboard Khunda. I'm going to find the geneticist," Lexy raised her hand as the others began to complain, "The Council left us no choice. If we show our faces on any enlightened planet they will arrest and charge us without a trial. I am going to find some leverage even if the lead comes from Apaleo. Anyone who doesn't want to be involved will be dropped off at the first jump station. I'll even tie you up, so you look innocent."

Chapter Eleven

Marcus ducked into the elevator next to Lexy, whose head was bent over her comboard reviewing the tweaks she made to Khunda's system permissions. He bounced on his toes telling her he was struggling to contain his opinion.

"I don't need this right now, Marcus."

"I'm not here to fight you on this," he responded with raised hands. "No matter how much I disagree with the *plan*."

Lexy sighed, she had spent the last hour dodging the rest of the crew after they all felt the need to tell her how much they disagreed with her plan. She offered them a chance to jump ship, but they all refused to leave.

"Mmm, okay, then what *do* you want?" she asked, lowering the board to give him her full attention.

Marcus looked at his feet, his posture reminding her of a child who had lost his nerve. All of the stress she was holding in her shoulders melted away as she recognized his shy side. In all of their time together Lexy had only ever seen him lose his nerve around her. Most of the time he put on a face of confidence and, at times, arrogance. She suspected that her ability to see through his shit was what caught his eye. The first thing she noticed about him was his ass, but after being stuck together for days on an outpost she got to know his sweet side. That's when she fell for him.

Lexy reached out and took his hand just as the doors opened. She smiled, letting go as she led the way into Khunda's engine room. To the right, transparent panels showed flashing lights and pipes carrying fluids vital to the ship's functions. Lexy turned left with Marcus on her heels. She stopped at the last door and placed her hand on the panel next to it. A red light scanned her palm.

"Vocal recognition password." Khunda's tone requested.

"Zephla is a pain in my ass," Lexy responded, holding back a grin.

The panel flashed green.

"I bet Z loves that," Marcus chuckled.

"He doesn't know," Lexy winked at him, " and you won't tell him, right?"

His blue eyes sparkled as they met hers, and his grin lit up his whole face, causing Lexy's heart to flutter. Instead of the fiery passion boiling up in her gut, she felt a sense of safety and security.

His expression shifted slightly, "Are you sure about this?" Marcus asked, breaking through Lexy's thoughts. "I mean, he did offer you up to that mercenary."

Lexy couldn't see another way. The truth disc she attached to Apaleo's neck meant that he believed in this Ancient Blood theory and that he has the location of the scientist.

This may all be a long shot, but it's the only shot we have.

"I trust that Lo's truth disc works, and that everything Apaleo told us he believes."

"Yes, but Lex, you're up against the Council and Royals. If they are hiding this Ancient Bloodline, then they won't hesitate to kill us."

"And if we do nothing, we spend our lives in hiding, always looking over our shoulders. I refuse to live like that. We did nothing wrong, yet here we are, labeled as the enemy."

Marcus sighed, "I agree with you. I just wanted to make sure you weren't jumping without looking."

Lexy turned to face him, "Of course, I'm not. I don't want to do this, but what other choice do we have?" she rested her hand on his chest, "I don't want us to end up in the same prison Adohan is rotting in. And no offense, but you're not made for that life."

"Neither are you, Lexy."

She giggled, "I don't know. I went to school on Earth. I can hold my own."

Lexy turned and walked into Khunda's core room. The twenty-foot oval room gave off a sterile feeling, as webs of blue glowing tubes snaked up the white walls like veins. Anyone new to the insides of a spaceship would feel like they were standing inside an organic body.

She headed for Khunda's core, a silver and white pedestal standing in the center of the room.

Marcus followed her. "So this is what a core room looks like," he asked, looking around in awe.

Lexy opened a panel near the floor. "The Wonder has a core room too, you know."

Marcus stared at Khunda's organic brain floating in the cylinder on top of the pedestal. Tiny wires lay across the grey surface as small impulses fired like lightning. The creation of bio-integrated systems gave modern ships the ability to learn and anticipate the needs of their crew. Each of the specimens would be harvested from willing donors that believed it was a way to live beyond death.

Marcus tapped the glass, "Yeah, but there is no reason for me to go there. I have a full crew, remember?"

His comment annoyed her. Of course, she remembered. She would have a full crew, too, if anyone wanted to work with an Earthling.

Lexy entered a series of symbols on the small keypad until the light to her right flashed. She walked around Khunda's brain and pulled out a green crystal cube.

"What's that?" Marcus asked.

Lexy stood, tossing and catching the cube one-handed. "This is Khunda's location signal. Which is now deactivated. Meaning even Ameran can't track us."

Marcus rested his elbow on the corner of the pedestal. "You really are amazing."

Lexy rolled her eyes.

He slid his hand behind her ear and pulled her in. His lips were soft, but the kiss was intense, sending goosebumps over every inch of her body.

Pushing on his chest just enough to keep her forehead against his, she whispered, "We have to get back upstairs. You know, stuff to do," she breathed inches away from his lips.

"First, say that you will go to dinner with me when we get out of this mess," he demanded.

Lexy smiled at his hopeful expression.

"Okay, but it better be classier than that hole-in-the-wall you took me to in the Leo constellation."

He chuckled. "That wasn't my fault. Z told me you loved that place."

Lexy scrunched her nose. "This time, don't ask Z for suggestions. He isn't your biggest fan, and the greys blend up all kinds of gross ingredients and call it gourmet, so how would he know about good food?"

Lexy took deep breaths as they made their way back to the bridge. Marcus always had a way of getting her all worked up. She was beginning to lose the will to fight her feelings. Possibilities of what her life with Marcus would look like floated through her head until they stepped onto the bridge. Ali and Z were having such an intense argument that they didn't even notice Lexy and Marcus had entered.

After listening to their incoherent rants for a moment, Lexy whistled to get their attention. "What's up, guys?"

Ali slumped against the console, crossing her arms. "Apaleo told us which planet to head to, and Z here refuses to believe that we may need some help from a contact you guys have down there."

Lexy set the cube in front of Z. "What planet and who's the contact?"

Z raised his hand. "Lex, we don't need-"

"Who, Z?"

Dropping his shoulders, Z answered, "Alpha Virgo, and it's Edward."

Lexy looked at Ali, not believing what she heard. She swore that she could die happy if she never set eyes on that spoiled Royal again.

"As in King Edward?" Marcus asked.

"That's the one," Z replied, as he slid the cube into his pocket, and avoided eye contact with Lexy.

"This oughta be good," Marcus snorted, taking a seat at the navigation station.

Lexy gripped the back of her captain's chair.

"I don't think we need his help. We will just locate this scientist, ask a few questions, and then leave. I'm not anticipating anything going wrong."

"You never do," Ali sighed.

"You might want to rethink your last statement, Lex," Trent commented as he entered the bridge.

The blood drained from Lexy's face when Trent sent a file from his comboard to the main screen. It was a news article, and in bold letters, it read:

ROGUE CTA CREW JOINS FORCES WITH REBELS
The CTA has an infestation of criminal employees. From Royal fugitive Apaleo of Aria to Captain Greggs of Earth and her

"Well, damn. Apaleo was right. They are trying to bury us," Z said.

Lexy laced her fingers behind her neck and dropped her chin. Her neck was tight, and she knew she needed the stretch. Taking deep breaths, she thought about how quickly the story had changed, they could have cleared up a misunderstanding in a chaotic attack. Now, the Council made its stance clear. They would stop at nothing to silence them all.

"Okay, well, that changes things. Z, do you think Edward will turn us in?" Lexy asked.

"No, he has his hesitations with the system as well, so if anyone is going to listen, it would be Eddy-boy."

Marcus laughed, "Eddy-boy?"

"And how many Royals are you friends with, Captain Fancy Pants? Or better yet, do you have any friends?"

"All right, cut it out, you two," Lexy snapped.

Z flipped Marcus the bird.

"Z, how do we get a hold of him? All of his communications are monitored, right?"

Z stretched his arms behind his head, propping his feet on the console, "Well, not all of his communications are monitored."

His smile was cocky, and Lexy didn't want to know why he had a personal line of communication with Edward.

Ali did. "Wait, you have a direct line to a King of an Alpha planet?"

"Yep."

"Why?"

Lexy put her hand on Ali's arm and responded, "You don't want to know the answer to that."

"Because," Z went on, "My man Edward and I enjoy a good night on the town. Grabbing drinks, meeting new people, and taking in a show."

Lexy rolled her eyes. "You mean getting shit-faced with random strangers and lap dances."

Z shrugged. "Yeah, that's what I said."

Lexy sighed. There were too many things that could go wrong by contacting Edward. For one, he could turn them in.

Z looked at her, his feet sliding off the console.

"You know he would help us, right? I've gotten to know him, and he has a good side. If we explain the situation, then I'm sure he would help."

Lexy thought about the last time she talked to him. He had given her the journal with the lock of hair and strange language as an apology for the mess he had caused which led to Lexy being caught, tortured, and nearly killed.

"Okay, Z. Make the call and make sure we can meet somewhere security and the Guard won't spot us. Don't tell him too much, though. He doesn't need to know we are chasing a conspiracy."

Z nodded and left the bridge.

Trent took Z's seat. "Are you sure about Edward?"

"No," Lexy answered truthfully. "I think I've learned that nothing is a sure thing, but we are going to need his help if we want to get anywhere on Alpha Virgo. Besides, if he tries anything, we can always use him as a bargaining chip."

Chapter Twelve

Lexy pulled the headscarf to cover more of her face. She and Z walked along the crowded stone-paved streets in the capital city of Alpha Virgo. Being known for its temples and churches meant the use of identifying tech was low, as the beings that lived on Alpha Virgo expected the Royals to keep religion a personal and private affair. That didn't mean that she and Z could move freely. They dodged multiple Guard members when they stepped off the "no questions asked" jump ship. The Royals must have increased security in the capital cities.

Various beings pushed past them as they weaved through the ancient streets. Many were devout to their religions as they wore head coverings similar to those Lexy and Z used to keep their faces hidden. Aqua beings of various shades of blue and green skin were covered with gold jewelry and seashells in order to keep them connected to the oceans. Plant hybrid beings with green-toned skin grew flowers in their hair, while some grew vines that twisted up their arms and legs. A group of Greys, shorter than Z, pushed passed with head coverings of a deep red. Lexy remembered that the more profound the shade of red the higher they ranked in their version of a church.

Alpha Virgo is often shrugged off as the planet of religious crazies. Lexy never saw it that way. Her aunt held a strong belief that religion and faith held people together through the bad times. And Lexy held a similar view. After her parent's death, she spent months studying the many faith systems. Lexy never settled on one but she was able to find some comfort in each. To her, Alpha Virgo will always be a sign of how every being is the same no matter their genetics.

Z led her toward a temple dedicated to the goddess of love. On Earth known as Venus, but out here she is known by many names.

I guess we're all not that different.

As they walked under the ornate arched doorway, Lexy leaned closer to Z. "This is the super secret meeting spot?"

Z huffed at her sarcasm, "Yeah. So?"

Paintings lined the walls of the temple entrance. The images of lovers in various poses caused Lexy to blush. She could see why this would be Edward's choice.

"Well, this seems about right," Lexy mumbled.

She followed Z into the main hall that resembled an ancient cavern with stone walls and an arched stone ceiling. The space was filled with couches and cushions that Lexy could only assume were for the more *pleasurable* things in life. While Lexy inhaled the vanilla-scented air she scanned the room. A mix of doors and curtains lined the outer walls. The far wall was lined with golden statues of the goddess with tables in front of each for offerings. The center golden form depicted Venus standing on the traditional clamshell, naked.

"Have you joined to this faith?" she asked Z, holding back a smirk.

Z led her toward a door on the left side of the main room. "You know the goddess Venus wasn't just about sex. She was about love and pleasure in all of its forms. Like that look you get in your eyes when you see one of your books in print for the first time." Z stopped in front of the door and knocked a rhythm she was unfamiliar with. "Or when you first adopted your dog, Bones. Remember, Lexy, a stereotype may be statistically true, but it isn't the whole truth."

Lexy leaned against the door frame, "Geez, when did you get so deep?"

His smile widened with an evil twinkle in his eyes. "While you were rekindling the flame with captain-fancy-pants."

Her back straightened and she took a deep breath before responding. "I know you hate him, but I believe that he really is sorry... I think I love him, Z."

She searched his face for a sign of how her confession landed. Z's eyes softened. "Lexy, you are my best friend and basically my sister, so if you love him and think he can make you happy, I will support you. I just have one question."

"What is that?" Her voice sounded hesitant out loud rather than the confidence she was trying for.

"What happened with Trent?"

"What about Trent?" she asked, rubbing her arm and staring at the engravings on the heavy wooden door, so he couldn't see into her eyes. Z was always good at seeing past her bluffs.

"Didn't you two have a dinner date planned? What happened with that?"

"For one, after the Royal mission when we got back to Earth, he had a lot on his mind. With just finding out aliens are real and becoming a member of a space crew. Not to mention, we work together on the same ship, so I don't think that would be a good idea." Lexy traced a flower carved into the door with her finger. "I also think something may be going on between him and Ali."

The last words dug into Lexy's gut in a way they shouldn't have, while Z's uncharacteristic silence made her squirm.

"Say something," she demanded.

"What do you want me to say?"

"I don't know. A snarky comment or something. You being sensible is worrying me."

He chuckled, "Maybe being in a holy place such as this makes me mature."

Lexy snorted.

"Or it could be that I'm team Trent." Z continued, "But I know how much you and Marcus care about each other. It may be annoying as hell, but I'm pretty sure I annoy you once in a while, too."

"Once in a while?" Lexy scoffed.

"What? I am the perfect best friend."

"Yes, you are."

The door lock clicked, and it swung inward. A hooded, hunched figure motioned them into the long hallway. *Now I know why it took so long to answer the door.* Z led her along the arched walkway that curved to the left and down a set of stone stairs. The further they walked the more Lexy felt uneasy about meeting deep inside a temple. Another intricately carved door stopped them from venturing any further. The figure slid past Lexy a little too close for comfort and unlocked the door with a key it pulled from its robes. The door opened, and to Lexy's surprise, the room was decorated for a King. Lexy's head snapped toward the figure. She snatched the hood off its face to reveal Edward's charming smile.

"Wonderful to see you again, Captain." He said, flipping his perfectly blonde hair out of his crystal blue eyes. He hadn't changed much in the time since they last saw each other. Edward stood a couple of inches taller than Lexy. His broad shoulders and muscular arms caught more than a few eyes.

Lexy pinched her brow and pushed past him into the room. She scanned over the silk sheets on the four-poster bed with sheer white curtains pulled to the corners to her left. To her right, an assortment of chairs, loveseats, and lounges were arranged into a circle with small tables between each of them. A large wardrobe sat against the far wall.

"Let me guess. *This* is your red room?"

Edward looked at Z confused. "No, it's blue, mostly."

Lexy shook her head and crossed her arms. "No, it's an Earth reference to a sex room."

The smile that crossed his face reminded her how much of a pain in the ass he was.

"Well, sex does indeed happen here, but it is more of an escape for me. If I need to get away from everything up there, I come here."

Lexy nodded. "Oh, yes. I can see how having your every need catered to could be distressing."

Edward threw himself into a chair. "That is why I like you, Captain Greggs. You always say what is on your mind. I can't trust anyone else to be honest with me."

Z took the chair across from him. "The novelty wears off after a while, but she has other good qualities, I promise."

Lexy took off her scarf and laid it on the chair before taking a seat. "For me, honesty and trust are the most important things in a relationship of any kind."

"I agree, Captain, which is why I am here. Z has become a trusted friend and, at times, an advisor."

Lexy turned to Z, her eyebrow raised in shock.

"What? I can be smart."

"Oh, I know you're smart but advising on Royal affairs, wow!"

Edward shifted to stand. "Would you like a drink, Captain?"

"No, thank you," she replied.

"I'll take a shot of–" Z started.

Lexy cleared her throat at him.

"Just hot tea if you've got it?" Z finished.

Edward began making the drinks on the cart against the wall. A king making tea was a bit unnerving. For a moment, she just watched him, imagining that he was just like any other man. She could admit that he was handsome with his square jaw and sandy blonde hair. And if she was younger and dumber, she would find it hard not to fall for his charms.

Edward handed Z his tea before returning to his seat. "So I hear you two have decided to defy the council and piss off the Royals."

Z choked on his tea. "Yes, well, you know how we do things."

"That is not what happened!" Lexy insisted.

Edward raised his glass at her. "I know. I have sources who told me about your agreement with the Council and the attack on Aria. Unfortunately, that is where my knowledge stops. Would you be so kind as to fill me in?"

Lexy glanced at Z, unsure of the finer details that Edward knew.

"Well, for one, the council cornered us into searching for Apaleo, which is why we were on Aria in the first place. But then the planet was attacked by a ship captained by a woman named Nala. Who, as far as I know, is still a member of the Guard. What I do know is that she is ruthless and cruel. I can assure you that leading that attack gave her great pleasure."

Lexy ground her foot into the carpet. She wanted another chance to shut Nala.

Edward looked at Z, who nodded. "So, I take it you decided to take on this woman and her crew by yourself."

Z laughed. "Now you're getting what it's like working with her."

Rolling her eyes, she said, "There were people being attacked and dying. There were children that the bombs could have killed if I hadn't helped. What did you want me to do, turn tail and run?"

"Like the Guard members stationed in the city?" Edward stated more than he asked.

His eyes held an understanding that filled Lexy with anger.

"Oh shit," she whispered, "I didn't even think about that."

Edward stood to return his glass to the drink cart. "No, you were a little busy dealing with Apaleo."

"Well, more like he saved her ass," Z responded as the realization washed over Lexy.

She stood and began pacing, which always helped her think.

"But why would the Guard leave during an attack? I know some of them look down on the warrior tribes, but to leave them to die is unimaginable."

"Maybe it wasn't by choice," Edward said, leaning on the back of Z's chair

Lexy stopped, making eye contact with Edward. "You sound as if you have more information than you're telling us. Is there something you would like to add? We are on a bit of a time crunch?"

He looked her up and down, making her skin crawl.

"My dear Captain, I am on your side, but like you, I am running on … oh, what is the Earth word for it? Ah!" Edward snapped his fingers. "A conspiracy theory."

Z's eyes shot to meet Lexy's. "I didn't tell him that!" he insisted.

Edward chuckled. "Z didn't say a word. I told you, I have my own sources."

Lexy's heart was hammering in her chest. She trusted that Z didn't tell him, but she had no idea where he would have heard that phrase. Her confusion must have been showing because Edward motioned for her to take a seat.

"I am on your side, and I will prove it. After you and your crew left me here on Alpha Virgo, I spent several days meeting with religious and spiritual leaders. You can guess how riveting these talks were. But during the last meeting, I met a woman–"

Lexy scoffed.

"Let me finish, Captain." Edward continued, "She was a priestess for the goddess Hecate. During our time together, she told me about the Ancient Blood theory. I dismissed it as a story told to give hope or explain why the Ancients left. Then one day, I was touring a lab nearby when I noticed a scientist who looked familiar. I couldn't place where I had seen her before."

"Did you bang her, too?" Lexy asked before she could stop herself.

"No," Edward sighed. "What makes you think I'm not still holding out for you, my dear Captain?"

Lexy couldn't tell if his tone was sarcastic or arrogant.

Z chuckled as he stood. "Sorry, Eddy, but Lex here has rekindled the flame with fancy man Marcus."

Lexy rolled her eyes as Edward's jaw dropped. It became clear that she may have been the topic of conversation on more than one occasion.

"Captain, what about his indiscretion?"

Lexy held up her hand. "Whoa, now. My private life is not the topic of this meeting. We have every member of the Guard looking for us, remember?"

Edward cleared his throat and returned to his chair.

"I asked around to the few I trust and found out that she was some sort of genius in her youth, but at some point, I guess she fell out of favor with the Council. My predecessor offered her a permanent lab, and she has been here ever since." He nodded toward Z. "It wasn't until Z sent me the message asking about a geneticist that I put the pieces together."

Lexy glanced at Z. What pieces? To what puzzle? Lexy felt like she taking a test she didn't study for. "Wait, what am I missing?"

Edward stood, taking the empty tea cup from Z and placing it on the drink cart.

"Captain, those who have some genius-level skill can only fall out of favor when they go against the wishes of the Council and Royals. So ..."

"... So she is the geneticist that found evidence of the Ancient Bloodline," Lexy finished. "But why hasn't this been leaked? Why isn't this out there as more than just a conspiracy?"

Z moved toward a tapestry near the back of the room. The image stitched on it was of a beautiful woman with dark hair and deep purple eyes. She wore pale blue cloth tied at her waist.

"Lexy, even you can't be so naive to think the news feeds tell us everything. Those who control the sharing of information, control the information."

He raised his hand and pulled the tapestry aside, revealing a stone wall. Lexy stood, wondering what he was up to as he leaned forward and pushed one of the stones inward. A section of the wall shifted backward and into the wall on the right. Lexy walked over to look through the opening. A long dark hallway stretched before her.

Edward walked up behind her, placing his hand on her lower back. "After you, my Captain."

She looked at him, taking in the details she had missed before. His skin looked older than when she last saw him, with wrinkles creeping in at the edges of his eyes. A couple of gray hairs were sprinkled just above his ears. His eyes still held the mischief of an adolescent, but something in them seemed changed. Almost mature.

"Where are we going?" she asked before she could stop herself.

She knew the answer, and something in her pulled with anticipation. Lexy felt excited and scared all at the same time without knowing why.

He smiled. "To meet the famed geneticist."

Chapter Thirteen

The tunnel ran under the city streets. At every turn, a grate above their heads let sunlight wash over them. Z led the way, but Edward called out turns for him to take. Lexy tried to recognize markings carved into the stone walls at each turn. Even with her impeccable grades in the language classes at the academy, the origin and meaning of the symbols eluded her.

At every step, her heart beat louder in her chest. *How did Edward know so much about the theory that she knew nothing about? Why would the Royals be so threatened by the discovery of an Ancient Bloodline?* According to the Royal history books, the Ancients left the Royals in charge of the Enlightened planets.

Unless the Royals wrote history that way.

Lexy shook her head. Am I really thinking this way? Apaleo and Nora believe the Bloodline theory is real – enough to risk their lives and the lives of others, but what would this discovery change?

Lexy rubbed the scar on her arm as they turned right again. The memory of Adohan's knife cutting into her skin made the hair on her neck stand on end. Apaleo had given Edward and her over to Adohan to get the location of the geneticist. In

Apaleo's eyes, their lives were worth the proof of the Ancient Blood theory.

Ahead of them, the tunnel narrowed as a stone staircase rose into the darkness. Lexy stopped. Frozen. *What if this gene is real? Is life ever going to go back to normal?*

Edward placed his hand on her back, causing her to jump. For a moment, she had forgotten he was there. He smiled and pushed her gently up the first few steps. They made their way up to what Lexy could assume would be street-level or higher. Z had to stop halfway up the stairs, huffing.

Lexy rolled her eyes, "Maybe a little less party life and a little more gym life," she mumbled.

"Whaa...nooo...I'm good," he puffed as he straightened and continued up the stairs.

The door at the top was carved out of stone and fit into the wall almost perfectly. A thin outline was the only giveaway that it was there. Edward eased around her. His touch was gentle. He must have sensed how tense she was. Taking a deep breath, she dropped her shoulders away from her ears.

Edward slid a thin 1x1-inch stone in until they heard a click. The stone sat to the right of the door and left Lexy wondering what they would find on the other side.

She didn't have long to wait as the stone slid back into its original position and clicked again. This time, the door swung toward them, causing them to squish together to stay out of its way. Light spilled into the darkness. Lexy's eyes adjusted, and a figure came into focus. It stood half as tall as Lexy, with an enlarged and elongated head. The body and limbs were thin, even under the black pants and blue blouse. The being before them was a Grey.

"Edward, you brought friends? I hope they aren't as easy as your normal crowd." Laughing, Lexy pointed to Z. "He is, but I'm here for some information."

Edward stepped forward and planted a kiss on the female gray's small cheek. She grunted at him and led the way into the room. Z and Lexy exchanged a glance before they followed.

They entered a small, curved room with two couches in the middle separated by a short table. It reminded Lexy of her Aunt May's formal sitting room, which no one used. The only difference was dusty picture frames that held sketches of DNA strands and chemical bonds rather than family photos. Lexy recognized some she had learned in her college chemistry classes, except these were more detailed.

Edward and the grey walked into the adjacent room, chatting about local news. Z looked over the sketches. Stopping in front of an image, he blew off the dust and squinted at it. He looked back at Lexy before taking the frame off the wall. Tucking it under his arm he walked into the next room.

"Okay, so I guess we are staying for a visit. It's not like we have people looking for us or anything," Lexy complained, trailing behind Z.

Lexy entered as Z took a seat at the solid wood table in the center of the room. Edward motioned for Lexy to take the seat between him and Z, as the grey woman pulled a small cake from the pantry.

Lexy looked around the kitchen. Metal appliances sat on the counter that lined the room. Above the sink, a window overlooked the neighborhood market. Books and papers were scattered across the center of the table. Pages filled with genetic codes and writing in various languages lay in small stacks. Sprinkled within the mess were images of artifacts Lexy had never seen before.

"Let me introduce myself," the grey said, breaking the silence. "My name is Innes. I am the head geneticist at the Alpha Virgo Royal Lab. According to the note Edward sent, you have some questions for me."

Lexy stared at Innes in silence. Now that she was in the moment, she couldn't think of anything to say. Sitting in front of the woman who claimed to have discovered the bloodline and the reason Apaleo gave Edward and Lexy over to Adohan was far more daunting than she thought it would be. Lexy shook herself, glancing at Edward.

"She is why Apaleo handed us over to be tortured and killed, and you're friends now?" Lexy asked, puzzled.

Edward shrugged. "She bakes a delicious cake." He took the slice of cake Innes handed him.

Z reached across Lexy, pulling a plate toward his seat. "I'll try some."

Lexy sighed.

"Okay, so we're friends now. Good. Great. This is fabulous." She pinched the bridge of her nose. "Hi, I'm Lexy. Captain of Khunda and wanted by the Guard for being too damn good at my job."

"I know who you are," Innes replied, passing Lexy a slice of cake. "You look just like your father."

Confusion must have crossed her face because Z put down his fork and tapped Lexy's elbow. He wiped his mouth on his sleeve before sliding the frame to her.

Lexy took it as Z pointed at the image in the frame. Lexy looked down at a sketch of people. People she recognized. Innes was much younger and stood in the front while four adults stood behind her. Two were Z's parents, and the others were Lexy's.

She tried to suck in air, but it caught in her throat. Tears filled her eyes as they shot to Innes, searching for an answer.

"You knew my parents? How...? When...?"

Edward handed her his napkin. She patted at the tears and took a deep breath. In the silence, a realization grew. Her heart began to ache as Innes started to speak.

"Your parents gave their lives to save me."

Lexy sat back in her chair. She never thought she would meet the "cargo" her parents were transporting when they were attacked. Lexy took the chance to look over Innes. Her eyes looked tired, and wrinkles creased her forehead.

Edward turned to face Lexy, resting his arm on the back of his chair.

"I know this is a lot to process, but we need our Captain to be clear-headed right now."

"I'm not your Captain," she whispered.

His smile revealed his dimples. "Yes, you are."

"I told you we could trust him," Z mumbled through a full mouth.

Lexy sat forward, picked up her fork, and cut into her cake. "Okay, tell me about the gene."

Innes smiled. "Before I rode with your parents, I worked at a lab for the Council." she explained, "At the time, I was working on deconstructing the modification the Greys had created on Alpha Leo."

"Apaleo's planet," Lexy commented, taking a bite of the delicious citrus cake.

"Yes. I found a group of highly concentrated genes in the junk DNA that wasn't present in the Royal's DNA," Innes said. "I started to cross-reference this with those native to Alpha Virgo, another Grey-created species, as you know, and found they have the same groups." Innes turned to put the leftover cake away. "That is how I met Edward's predecessor. When I told the Speaker of the Council about the link, I found myself blocked from the sample database. I was told I was being sent to a lab in the outer region to work on another project. I was young, and I couldn't understand why they would block me from such a find. As you can guess, it upset me. Your parents were the ones charged with transporting me. While onboard, they took care of me as if I was their own. I never had parents, so I didn't know what it felt like to be cared for."

Lexy cleared her throat in an attempt to swallow the lump that formed. "They were always there for me too," she whispered.

Z pushed his plate toward the center of the counter and wiped his hands on a napkin. "I appreciate the walk down memory lane, but we are in a hurry, so tell us about this Ancient Blood thingy."

Lexy snorted. "He's right. We need information we can use to keep the Council from killing us."

"If that is even possible," Edward retorted.

Lexy searched his face for a sign that he might know more than he was telling them. Edward stared at Innes as she began to speak. Lexy knew he was trying to avoid her eyes.

"My theory is that the Ancients used the Grey's genetic alterations to hide some of their own DNA," Innes stated just before she slipped past Edward and ducked her head into a cabinet behind them.

"Why would they do that?" Lexy asked, shifting to watch as Innes dug a backpack out and filled it with papers and a notebook from the table. Lexy picked up a photo of a stone tablet with what she could guess were words carved onto it. The symbols looked familiar, but not from any of her classes. Innes finished stuffing the bag with the last of the images and placed it on her back.

"I don't know." Innes replied, "Without more samples from the Grey planets, I can't prove the connection, let alone find the similarities and what they mean."

Innes' small form hunched, twirling a thin silver band on her wrist.

"Innes?" Edward's sharp tone stopped Lexy's heart.

Innes gripped the band and slid her hand out of the ring with a scream. The band left deep tears in her skin where blood began oozing from. The small woman looked back up at Lexy. "Now, you have to take me with you."

Lexy stood as Edward grabbed a towel off the counter and wrapped it around Innes' now bleeding hand.

"What?" Realization washed over her. The silver band was a Royal tracking band, which when removed, alerted every Gruard in the area.

Edward faced Lexy. "You have to go! Take Innes. Get her to Apaleo. He will know where to go."

"What are you talking about?" Lexy asked, "We just came here for answers. If we take her, they'll think we kidnapped her."

Z, who had ducked into the room they came from, came running back into the kitchen. "Guards are heading into the building. We have to go, Lex!"

Lexy felt like she had been caught in a tornado. Nothing made sense. "Wait!"

Z slid his arm around Innes and began steering her back toward the hidden door. Edward pushed Lexy after them.

"Go. I can stall them," Edward said, "You're going to have to run. Keep her safe. I know you will."

The last words brought Lexy's eyes to meet his. The spoiled, horn dog she knew was no longer there. His eyes held fear, but it wasn't for himself. He was worried about them.

"Why are you doing this?" Lexy asked, her hands gripping the frame of the stone door.

"For my people and for yours," Edward said, placing his hands on her cheeks and touching his forehead to hers. "Be safe, my Captain."

He pushed her gently down the first few stairs and pulled the door closed.

Chapter Fourteen

They ran through the tunnels as the sunlight above them flashed as they passed under each grate. Z led the way, holding Innes' uninjured arm. Lexy brought up the rear, looking behind her at every sound.

The tunnels dumped them into a large cave near one of the less reputable docks. Z climbed the stone stairs that led toward the jump ship that dropped them off on Alpha Virgo. "I figured we would need a quick getaway, so I asked these guys to hang out here for a while."

Lexy held her breath as she passed the jump ship's captain.

The ride back was smelly and the unwashed crew kept looking at Innes' blood-stained bandage, Lexy was thankful Z had arranged it. "You know sometimes your questionable dealings come in handy," she whispered to him as the darkness of space flooded into the small ship. Z lived without fear, while Lexy felt stuck most of the time.

As she watched Z sitting next to Innes a feeling sank into her gut. *What if I lived my life chasing a third Captain's Star, and now I never get it? What will I do if we survive?*

There was a strange ease in her shoulders. But she had no time to question it as the rickety ship landed. Lexy followed Z and Innes down the ramp and onto their jump ship hidden in a crater on the moon of a dead planet. The ramps were close enough to connect the ship's outer energy fields, making them safe to cross.

They seemed to settle into the quiet calm as the jump ship flew back to *Khunda*. Z cleaned and wrapped Innes' hand. Luckily, Grays had three fingers and a thumb, so the damage from ripping off her tracking band was minimal. Lexy sat at the ship's console, thinking through her options. There weren't many.

First, we could dump Innes, Apaleo, and Nora on the nearest planet, but that wouldn't stop the Counsel from throwing us in prison or killing us. Second, we could hand all three of them over to the Counsel and try to explain our innocence. Freedom didn't seem likely in that scenario either. Which, left the last option. We figure out if the Ancient gene is real and use the information as leverage to clear the air. But will that be enough?

Lexy walked back to the jump ship's rear hold, where Z was clearing up the medical supplies while Innes cradled her newly bandaged arm.

"So, then this aqua breed sat next to me and asked if she could buy me a drink, haha. I thought sure, why not? I haven't been with a fish before." Z laughed, not noticing the disgust on Innes' face.

Lexy leaned on the halo table. "Wow, Z, that may be too much information for our new friend."

He looked up at Innes with her large almond eyes somehow wider in discomfort. "Yeah so ... uh...we can clean your hand up better...uh when we get back," Z mumbled as he threw the rest of the supplies into the bag and hurried toward the front of the ship. Lexy had never known him to shy away from making people uncomfortable.

She decided that she better take this time to ask some questions before the others were around.

"What do you need to find the link between the Gray planets?"

Innes looked from Z back to Lexy. "I need some blood samples from two of the three Gray-created beings: Earthling and Alpha Leo. Edward helped me acquire some samples from natives of Alpha Virgo."

"Then what?" Lexy pushed.

"Then I need a lab. Nothing huge. Just enough for me to isolate the section of DNA I need to compare. The samples must be native to the planet to rule out any other possible sources for a link. When I have three samples that all have the link, I have to find more samples to confirm it. But I have to stay alive first. That is where you come in, Captain."

Lexy stood up. "What? No. I'm not a bodyguard."

"Then find me someone who is."

"You're a bit demanding for someone on the run."

Innes's face softened. "I hate to break it to you, but you're on the run too."

The words hit Lexy in the gut. She may have toed the line from time to time, but she always prided herself on being one of the good guys, always on the side of the Counsel and the Royals. A realization washed over her, that her need to prove herself may have kept her from being open to their faults. Memories of her time in the Guard flashed by. There were missions she began to question if they were given the whole story. *How much did we aid in the Council's overstep? Why didn't I ask more questions?*

"I'm starting to realize that." Lexy pinched her nose. "Well, I'm sure Apaleo and Nora will give you blood. I mean, Apaleo did hand Edward and me over to die just to get your location."

Lexy placed her hand on the halo table's control pad, bringing it to life. The holographic image of the Enlightened planets faded into view above the table.

Lexy waved her hand at the mass of planets.

"Where would you like to go? We will drop you off anywhere you want."

Innes stood looking over the image. Then, walking to the other side of the table, she scanned each planet. Lexy knew she was reading through the names that appeared.

"Here." Innes proclaimed, pointing to a planet on the far end of Royal's control. Lexy looked at the largely blue ball, its name popping up next to it.

"That is an inhabited planet." Lexy walked to stand next to Innes, using her finger to enlarge and isolate the planet. "It says here that it was deserted after the Gray war. It only has one land mass with limited access to fresh water."

"I want to go there," Innes pressed.

"One minute till we dock with *Khunda*," Z called from the front.

"Buckle in. We'll talk about it after we land," Lexy ordered, heading to sit next to Z.

"Thank you," Innes called after her.

Lexy glanced back, giving her a weak smile.

"I've sent our authorization code to *Khunda* and let Trent know we have a passenger," Z filled her in as she buckled herself into the secondary pilot seat. Darkness surrounded them, except for the light from the jump ship's front beams bouncing off the walls of the cave where *Khunda* was hidden.

"Good. Do you know of a way to get to the Draco planets without using any registered jump stations?"

"I'm sure I do. Why? You thinking about moving?"

"No," she responded. "Innes wants to go to a planet on the far end of Draco."

Z glanced back at Innes. "Why? I heard most of the planets were decimated in the war."

"I don't know, but we can talk it over with the others."

Khunda came into view, making Lexy relax in her seat. In just a few minutes, she would be back on her ship with the rest of her friends, figuring out how to fix this mess.

The jump ship hummed as it came to rest on *Khunda's* cargo bay floor. "Let's do the damn thing!" Z hollered as he turned off the engine and hopped out of his seat.

Lexy led the way down the ramp and into Ali's open arms.

"I am so glad you made it back alright," Ali said, giving Lexy a final squeeze before letting go.

Trent came to stand next to Lexy. "Who is your passenger?"

"Oh, that is one hell of a long story. Let's get out of the Virgo planets first."

The sound of laser weapons charging up pulled Lexy and Trent's focus behind them. A group of ten beings in brown jackets stretched out across *Khunda's* ramp, all with weapons raised and pointed at them.

Where the hell did they come from?

Lexy pushed Ali behind her as she pulled her energy pulse weapon from its holster, tucked in her waistband. Trent already had his pulse weapon raised, taking in all ten pointed back at them.

An aqua breed in the center of the group broke the silence. "I think it would be smarter for you to lower *your* weapons."

"How did you get past *Khunda's* exterior sensors?" Lexy demanded.

Several chuckles bounced off the cave walls. The elevator doors opened, drawing the attention of the group. Marcus walked out, raising his hands as he took in the scene.

Two intruders rushed toward him, searching for weapons as more walked up the ramp. The aqua breed motioned for Lexy and Trent to lower their weapons. Lexy met Trent's eyes, noticing his reluctance, but not knowing what other options they had. She began to lower her arm, and Trent followed. More intruders rushed forward, patting down each of them and taking their weapons. A barrel was shoved into her back, pushing her into the open space of the cargo bay. Marcus came to stand on one side of Lexy while Trent stood on the other. Ali and Z joined them after being searched and shoved in their direction.

Innes must have gone invisible, a survival skill that evolved over centuries of genetic tweaking.

"Where is your leader?" Lexy called to the blue-skinned man. His neck gills fluttered open and closed. "Because I know your ugly ass isn't in charge."

The man's lips curled to reveal pointed teeth.

"No. He isn't," called a familiar, cocky voice. Lexy watched as Nala sauntered up *Khunda's* ramp. The woman dripped arrogance from her braided blonde hair to her spiked boots.

Bitch.

"I don't remember inviting you," Lexy spat between gritted teeth.

"Captain Greggs, I don't give a fuck. Have you not figured that out by now." Nala looked around the cargo bay, as several of her crew members began searching the bay, dumping the contents of supply boxes onto the bay floor.

What are they looking for? Innes?

"Captain Nala, the elevator won't open," called a woman standing by the keypad.

Nala sighed, looking over Lexy and the others. Her eyes narrowed at Ali.

"You don't look like combat is your thing. You must be the tech queen. Be a dear and open the elevators."

"No," Ali spat back.

Nala's face twisted, and two tattooed plant breeds grabbed Ali's arms. Lexy and Trent jumped at them surprising the beings that formed a loose circle around Khunda's crew. Lexy punched the green-skinned being before he landed a blow into Lexy's gut. She doubled over as her opponent threw her to the floor, coming to stand over her with a laser aimed at her head. Trent wrestled with the now bloody-faced man near the bay doors. The sound of a weapon discharging near the back of the bay drew the attention of her attacker. Lexy took the opportunity to throw her legs upward and wrapped them around his arm, she twisted, pulling her opponent down with force. A loud thud told her that his head had made contact with the metal floor. She sat up, snatching the pistol from his now relaxed hand. Shifting to one side, she took in the chaos that had erupted. Trent and Marcus each fought several brown coats. Ali had acquired a weapon she now used to shoot anyone within range. The only indication of Z's actions was a trail of bodies leading toward the cell doors.

To Lexy's surprise, Nora and Apaleo were taking down several intruders in the back of the bay.

Z must have let them out. Holy shit, they're kicking ass.

Lexy took down two beings as Nala raised a weapon and pointed it toward Marcus. Shock and then anger shot through Lexy as she took aim, letting her breath out just before she squeezed the trigger. A pulse hit Nala's pistol causing a small explosion.

Lexy shifted her aim and squeezed the trigger again, but the weapon didn't fire. It was out of juice. She stood and sprinted to Nala, who was cradling her burned hand. Nala sneered as she tried to block Lexy's strike, failing and falling to the floor. As Lexy closed the small space between them, Nala swung her leg out, catching Lexy's legs. As she collided with the ground, all the air left Lexy's lungs, stunning her just long enough for Nala to regain her footing. She stood over Lexy with a triumphant smile.

"They want you alive, but I'll just tell 'em you left me no choice." Nala raised her foot and brought it down hard, aiming for Lexy's throat, but Lexy rolled fast onto her left side and then back, wrapping her arm up Nala's leg. Lexy rolled again with all her strength, forcing Nala to fall over her. She released Nala's leg and pushed up into a fighting stance. Nala had ended up halfway down the ramp. They stared at each other, waiting for the other to make the first move.

"Fuck it," Lexy whispered, advancing on Nala, who shifted toward one side.

"Do you think you can beat me, Captain Greggs?"

"As I recall, I've kicked your ass before."

Nala narrowed her eyes, "Only because that pervert of a pilot helped."

Lexy shrugged. "A win is a win."

Lexy heard Ali call out in pain. She turned her head without thinking giving Nala the chance she needed. Closing the gap between them in two long strides, Nala sank her knee into Lexy's gut. Lexy hit the metal floor, sliding to the edge of the ramp. The power of the energy field that kept them from being sucked into space, buzzed in her ears. Lexy coughed uncontrollably, unable to force her body to move. Nala came to stand over Lexy, raising her arm to point a newly acquired laser pulse gun at her head.

"Any final snarky remarks?" Nala hissed.

"Go to hell," Lexy wheezed.

"You first, Capt–"

A laser pulse hit Nala in the leg, dropping her to her knees. Lexy sat up, jabbing her fist into Nala's throat, causing her to choke and sputter. Lexy crawled back up the ramp as Nala flailed and gasped for air. Two strong arms looped under Lexy's, helping her to her feet. Lexy turned to see Marcus' cut and bloody face. She reached up to touch his cheek but hesitated.

"I'm okay, Lexy." his voice was calm, "Better than her," he nodded at Nala's now motionless body.

"She had it coming," Lexy stated.

Marcus chuckled.

Innes appeared next to them with a weapon in her hand, "I shot her." Her voice gave away her shock.

Lexy looked from Innes to Nala's body, "You're a pretty good shot."

Innes shrugged, "Not really. I was aiming for her head."

Lexy looked around the cargo bay. Ali and Trent were picking up weapons and setting them on the boxes along the railing. Z and Apaleo had started to drag bodies toward the ramp. Nora was pulling the emergency medical kit off the wall.

Lexy wrapped Marcus in a hug, "I love you," she whispered into his ear.

He pulled back, smiling at her. "I've always loved you."

She kissed his cheek, inhaling his musk, before turning to help with the cleanup. A slight feeling of relief fell over her. But it didn't last. Someone shoved her to the ground before a deafening bang echoed off the cargo bay's walls.

"No!" Innes cried out.

The horror in Innes' voice stilled Lexy's heart. She turned to see Marcus standing behind her. *He shoved me.* Confused, Lexy followed Marcus' gaze to the center of his chest, where blood was now spreading its way through his shirt.

"No!" she screamed, standing to catch him as he fell, "No. No. No. Stop!"

She lowered him onto the floor, pressing her hands into his chest in an attempt to stop the bleeding.

Trent rushed to the ramp, firing two shots into Nala's head.

Tears streamed down Lexy's face. "No. Don't leave me," she begged.

She looked into his eyes, but they stared lifelessly up at the ceiling. Then, cupping his face in her hands, she pressed her lips to his.

"Please, I love you," she said as tears dripped from her chin.

Lexy searched his face for any sign of life, but there was none. His eyes didn't sparkle for her. His hands wouldn't hold her again.

"No, please," she pleaded into the silence.

Looking up at her friends, she was shocked as they all stood there, doing nothing.

"Why aren't you doing anything? Help! Do something," Lexy demanded, pressing her forehead to Marcus'.

Ali knelt across from her, and tears slid down her pale cheeks. She rested her hand on Marcus' shoulder before raising her chin.

"May the Goddess hear me. Release this spirit and calm his soul," Ali spoke in a soft tone.

Lexy recognized it. In elven tradition, the prayer was spoken over the dead. The vice on her heart tightened.

"No," Lexy's voice cracked, "He isn't dead.

Z and Innes stood at Marcus' feet. Their heads bowed and hands on their hearts. The posture was a sign of respect among the Greys.

"No," she whispered, dropping back as the painful truth sank in.

Chapter Fifteen

Lexy ran her thumb along the top of Marcus' hand. His skin felt cold and hollow. His soul was gone, if living things had souls.

Trent and Apaleo had moved Marcus' body to a bed in the med room. Lexy asked them to leave him uncovered for a little longer. Trent agreed, and the crew went about cleaning out the cargo bay. Time had passed, but Lexy didn't know how long. Unable to let go of his hand. Unable to move from the cold stool. She brushed a tear off her cheek, wondering if the ache in her chest would ever dull.

Her thoughts were unfocused and hard to isolate.

How did Nala and her crew find us?

Should I contact Ameran to tell her about Marcus?

What do I do about Innes?

Lexy looked out of the clear wall that separated the cargo bay from the med room as Innes helped Trent carry the orphaned weapons to the repair room. Ali and Nora sprayed down the bay floor. Lexy looked from Innes to the blood-streaked metal. Innes needed samples. Lexy released Marcus' hand and began searching the drawers and countertop of the med room. She found sample bags, a collection kit, and shears. Placing her findings on the rolling table beside Marcus, Lexy paused, taking a shaky breath, before rolling up her sleeve and pressing one end of a blood collection tube against her skin. Taking a deep breath, she watched as the clear tube filled with her blood. Once it finished, she shoved it into a sample bag and marked the front with her name.

The easy part was over. She turned to Marcus' body.

"I hope you understand what I'm doing," she whispered.

Grabbing the shears, she cut away a section of his blood-stained shirt. Lexy held the fabric for a moment before sealing it in a plastic sample bag. She labeled the bag and pushed the now messy table toward the counter.

Lexy took a moment to give Marcus' hand one more squeeze before she left the room. She headed toward Innes, whose eyes widened as Lexy moved toward her.

"Here, two Earthling samples," she paused to settle her voice as Innes reached out to take the samples, "Marcus' mother was from Earth."

The air thickened as the rest of the crew took notice of the exchange. Lexy refused to look into their faces. The faces of her friends. She knew she would fall apart again if she saw one speck of pity in their eyes.

"Everyone on my crew is free to choose for themselves if they want to give a sample, but first, I want a report. How were they able to sneak up on us?"

Ali stepped forward, grabbing a comboard off a nearby crate. "Their ship has advanced cloaking tech– so advanced I've never seen anything like it."

She handed the board to Lexy, who began swiping through the data Khunda's sensors had collected from Nala's ship. Ali was right: the cloaking tech was beyond what modern ships were equipped with, Lexy doubted Lo, the CTA's tech and supplies director, had seen anything like this. She searched the time stamps.

"Who started these scans?"

Ali shifted her weight.

"We think Marcus did before he left the bridge."

The corners of Lexy's eyes began to burn and the weight in her chest doubled.

Clearing her throat, she handed the board back to Ali, whose eyes searched Lexy's face. Knowing that elf breeds could read a person's emotions through eye contact, Lexy turned away. It wasn't the result she wanted. She found herself looking at Apaleo.

"Who let you out?"

"Um, that would be me," Z answered. "I figured we could use the help when shit hit the fan, sooo..."

Lexy raised her chin. "A lot of good that did."

Apaleo opened his mouth to respond but closed it as soon as Lexy raised her eyebrow.

"That's what I thought. Put them back in the cells."

The sound of Trent's weapon charging drew Apaleo and Nora's attention.

"Wait," Nora placed her hand on Lexy's shoulder, "We–"

Lexy grabbed her hand, twisting it and placing her free hand on Nora's shoulder to apply pressure, causing Nora to bend in half to avoid the pain.

Apaleo's face was flooded with rage, but his tone showed restraint.

"I know that you are upset, Captain, but we are not the reason Marcus is dead."

"Oh, you're not? Because last time I checked, you're the son-of-a-bitch that tossed Edward and me to the mercenaries, you're the reason the Counsel tricked us into hunting you down, and you're the reason Nala and her crew attacked us. Don't you dare stand there and claim innocence."

"I never claimed to be innocent, unlike you. You think your hands are clean? How many missions were you told not to talk to the cargo? How many missions did you run with boxes full of something you never asked questions about? Whether you like it or not, you have always been the Royal's mule. Why do you think I asked to be put on your crew for so many missions? I wanted to get closer to you, to keep an eye on you. You've always been on the Council's list because of your parents. Because they saved her," Apaleo spat, pointing to Innes.

Lexy released Nora, her blood boiling as Apaleo's words settled. She bolted forward, slamming her palms into his chest, shoving him backward. Lexy shoved him again and again.

"Hit me! If you think I'm one of them, then end me now. You have the chance." She struck his face. "Why won't you fight?" she screamed.

Apaleo caught her hand before her second swing could land. He turned her, pulling her into him. Wrapping his arms around her, he squeezed just enough to prevent her from doing any harm. She struggled against his grip, but he was stronger.

Lexy began to lose her fight.

"Marcus is dead. Nothing can bring him back. But look at your crew," Apaleo demanded.

Lexy looked up, seeing the fear and pain in the eyes of her friends. What little resolve Lexy had left was gone, and tears began streaming down her cheeks again.

Apaleo lowered his voice so that only Lexy could hear him, "Look at your friends. They are alive, and the path you decide to take will decide their fate. Will you give up and face life in prison or death? Or will you fight for your freedom? All of our freedom."

Lexy shook her head. "I can't. I can't lose them."

Trent, who began tapping his weapon on his leg as a warning to Apaleo, stepped forward, reaching his hand out to Lexy. "You made your point. Now, back in the cell."

Lexy took Trent's hand and reached for his gun. Confusion crossed Trent's face, but he let her take it.

Lexy took a settling breath. "No. Apaleo is right. We have to fight."

Trent stepped closer to her. "We can just go home. Earth is a neutral planet. They can't come for us there."

Lexy smiled at him. "I know, but I won't live my life hiding from them."

She squeezed Trent's hand, before passing him to address the rest of her crew.

"You can all decide for yourselves, but my parents died protecting her," Lexy nodded at Innes, "I know they would want me to do what is right– not what is easy."

They all looked at each other, silent conversations through looks and nods.

Nora spoke first, "Over all the years that Apaleo and I have suffered under Royal rule, he always spoke of his captain being the best at getting the job done. So, if anyone can do this, I believe it is you, my captain."

Lexy cocked her head at Nora's final words. Edward's words.

Apaleo passed Lexy to stand beside Nora. "I am yours to command, my captain."

Ali smiled at Lexy. "I stand with you, my captain."

Z hopped up to sit on a crate. "Well, you know I'm in... my captain."

Trent stood next to Lexy. "I feel like I'm missing something."

Lexy wiped a tear from her eye as connections started to come to light.

"Edward calls me that."

"Huh," Trent put his hands on his hips. "That royal pain-in-the-ass must not have been as dumb as I thought he was. Can we trust him?"

"I trust Z and Ali," Lexy responded.

"Okay, so what do we do next?"

Lexy shook her head. "That's not my call."

"Who…" Trent stopped himself, following Lexy's eyes which had landed on Innes.

"Innes. Where are we going?"

Shock crossed Innes' oversized, black eyes. She began fidgeting with the sample bags and shifting her weight from side to side. Z slid off the crate and came to stand next to Innes.

"It's okay," he told her in a calming voice, "If you trust Edward, you can trust us."

Lexy had only ever heard Z speak that way to animals and once to Lexy after she was told about her parents' death.

Lexy sighed. "Innes, if we are going to have a chance at surviving the Council's attacks, it will be because you were able to finish your work. So, tell us what you need."

Innes looked around at the group.

"I need a lab and samples. I need somewhere I can do my work in peace, without the Council keeping an eye on my tests."

"We can provide that," Apaleo spoke up, "Years ago, when Lexy's parents were transporting you, those in the rebellion built a lab for you when they heard about your findings that support the theory that could protect the Gray planets."

Innes shifted her weight from side to side. "Edward told me about the rebels and the lab. Will I be safe there?"

Nora nodded, "Yes, Apaleo and I were directed to get you, safely, to the lab, which is located on a rebel stronghold. We swore to keep you safe at all costs, because we know what your work could mean to those who cannot escape the Royal's control."

Lexy watched as Innes' eyes focused on the sample in her hand. Her elongated forehead pinched in thought. "Okay, I will go with you."

Lexy stepped forward, picked up the comboard, and cleared the screen. She handed it to Ali.

"Can you wipe and reprogram Nala's ship so we can use it?"

"On a normal ship, of course, but that ship is far more advanced."

"I wonder how Nala got a hold of so much advanced tech," Z said sarcastically. "Oh wait, I know, she was a puppet of the Royals to spread fear and lies to justify their actions."

Z rolled his eyes. Innes laughed, and Z's shoulders stiffened. Lexy made a mental note to mock him for his awkwardness around Innes.

Ali's head was already bent over the board. "I will see what I can do, and at least, I can get a better idea of what they are working with."

"Khunda," Lexy called out.

"Yes, captain," the soft tone of the ship answered.

"Extend all sensors and alert us if anyone comes within range. And I am giving Ali access to all systems."

"Voice Security code, please."

"Z is a pain in my ass," Lexy smirked as the others struggled to hide their chuckles.

"That's your security code. Wow. Don't worry. I'll change mine later." Z walked up the jump ship's ramp. "I'm going to check on some things."

Lexy cleared her throat. "Apaleo, where do you need to go?"

Apaleo glanced at Nora, who nodded back at him. Lexy saw a flash of softness in their eyes. Their love for each other had lasted this long with so many obstacles. She envied what they had.

"We have a safe house near here. I can give you the coordinates."

Lexy looked at Trent. "Can you take Apaleo and review the coordinates and see what jumps we'll have to make? You can ask Z if you need help finding any that aren't regulated or watched by the Royals." Trent nodded and stepped toward Apaleo. Lexy grabbed his arm. "Just in case," she said, handing Trent his weapon.

Trent nodded. As he and Apaleo walked toward the repair room, Z came bounding out of the jump ship.

"Lexy, there is a message from Lo."

Shocked, she reached for the comboard he was holding toward her.

"We are supposed to be silent, Z; the Guard can trace CTA messages."

Z shook his head. "Not this one. Lo and I set up a system of getting information to each other if shit went south. And it has, big time."

Lexy grabbed the board and pushed the start button on the message. Lo's face filled the screen.

"Z, I'm sending this because the Guard raided the CTA and arrested several beings. Dude, it's bad. They arrested Ameran."

Lexy covered her mouth in shock.

"It's all over the news waves. The Council is accusing Ameran of using the CTA to help the rebels. They are calling anyone who speaks out against the Counsel extremists. Some of the tech guys and I were able to get out, and we've gone into hiding. I've heard rumors. They're saying someone has been on your tail since you left Alpha Orion. Be careful. You have to hide–"

The feed froze. Lo's face twisted in fear. He had already been through so much at the hands of the Royals. He had been imprisoned after the Gray War and tortured. When the courts finally ruled that not all of the grays agreed with the genetic experiments being done, he was freed but not without scars. Inside and out. Lo never talked about it, but the still image on the comboard showed the pain and fear he held inside for years.

Lexy's anger pushed its way up. Her grip on the board tightened. She glanced around her to find everyone was frozen, staring at her. Waiting.

They will pay for this.

"Z, prep Khunda. We are getting to that safe house now. Trent. Apaleo. Go with Z." Lexy handed Z the comboard as the three of them ran toward the elevator.

"Nora, go through these crates, take what you will need for the three of you to get to the safe house, and load it onto the jump ship. Khunda, scan Nala's ship. I want to know everything there is to know about it before we blow it up. Ali, get whatever information you can from that ship as well. I want to know who Nala's contact was, how they were communicating, and how they traced us. Get whatever information you can from that ship. Innes come with me. I have a gift for you."

Lexy fumed as she led Innes to her quarters. There, she collected a flat, round device the size of a quarter from under her mattress and the book Edward had given her.

"In your apartment, I glanced at the pictures you had on the table. There were symbols like this," Lexy opened the book and showed Innes the elegant writing, "You were reading it, weren't you?"

Innes traced the edges of the page. "How did you get this?"

"Edward gave it to me. He said it was an apology for the mission he messed up."

"May I?" Innes asked. Lexy handed the book over to her. "This is far more detailed and intricate than I have ever seen," Innes squinted at the pages as she turned them cautiously. "It seems like a personal journal or diary."

Lexy shrugged. "Edward said it belonged to a woman from Alpha Virgo."

Innes flipped through the pages until she found the lock of hair. Picking it up, she turned it in her fingers, looking at Lexy questioningly.

"I don't know. It was in the book. Maybe hers or someone she loved."

Innes replaced the hair, closed the book, and hugged it to her chest.

"Thank you. Maybe it can give us some idea about her life and if she knew anything about the ancients. At the very least, it can help unlock more about the language. I just know enough to understand bits and pieces. There are no sources on it."

Lexy held out the metal device. "Take this too. Z gave it to me a long time ago. It's an untraceable communicator. If you need anything, just squeeze it and speak into it. I will get the message, and no one can trace it."

Innes slid the device in between the pages of the book and placed the book in her backpack.

Lexy smiled at her, knowing she would finish what her parents started. The mission they died for.

Alarms rang throughout the ship. Lexy and Innes covered their ears at the piercing sound.

Khunda's voice filled the room, "Captain, two Guard ships are approaching the moon."

Chapter Sixteen

Lexy squeezed through the door to the bridge as it opened. Alarms rang out while lights spun across the walls. She pointed Innes to the fold-out chair on the wall to their left of the navigation station. Innes quietly sat down and buckled herself in, hugging the journal.

"Z, how the hell did the Guard get here so fast?" Lexy called as she sat at the console.

"No clue, but my guess is Nala gave them a heads-up. *Khunda*, could you turn off those damn alarms."

Lexy's ears hummed from the alarms as she entered the commands for *Khunda* to start the engine and charge the weapons. She hoped they wouldn't have to fight the incoming ships, but the way their luck ran, it was inevitable.

Ali rushed onto the bridge. "I found a secure communication from Nala's ship to the closest Guard station. She was undoubtedly working under orders."

Lexy's eyebrows pinched. Having irrefutable evidence of the corruption hit her harder than she believed it would.

"*Khunda*, close the bay door and divert all nonessential system power to the shields."

"Yes, Captain."

Trent and Apaleo rushed onto the bridge.

"Weapons?" Trent asked Lexy, heading to his favorite chair on the right.

"Yep. Be ready to fire, but aim to disarm, not kill."

Apaleo groaned, causing Lexy to turn in her chair to look him in the eyes.

"I get that you have no issues with killing, but me and my crew are not murderers. Aim to disarm. Are we clear?"

Apaleo's arm muscles twitched, clearly not used to being put in his place. He nodded at Lexy and sat in the weapons chair next to Trent.

Lexy turned to Ali. "Were you able to get anything off that ship?"

"Yes, the tech may be new, but the systems are still basic Royal codes. The same codes I hacked when I was seven."

Lexy rolled her eyes. "Governments are the same on any planet, huh?"

"I will have the system files copied in two minutes. Then you can blow up the ship."

Lexy looked at Z, who shrugged.

"I can wait. Can the trigger-happy rebel handle it?" Z asked, wagging his thumb toward Apaleo.

Lexy sat back in her chair, running through the final takeoff checks. "He can and he will, or I will shoot him myself."

A low grumble behind her told Lexy that Apaleo was holding back his opinions. Lexy refused to turn around. Apaleo had sworn to be under her command, so she knew he would follow her orders. The warrior tribes had a deep sense of duty.

Khunda began to rumble far beneath their feet. The slight shift in the ship's internal gravity told her that the grounding locks had lifted. They were hovering just off the cave floor. *Khunda* waited, giving off a low hum, for Z's control to send them into space. The crew sat silent, waiting for Lexy's orders.

"Z, take us to the cave's entrance but keep us out of view. Trent, lock on to the engine of Nala's ship. Wait for my command."

Khunda floated forward, the darkness shifting as they left the depth of the dead moon. Lexy's heart beat faster as she realized this was their last chance to finish this mission. The mission her parents started so many years ago.

Lexy keyed in the command for *Khunda's* long-distance scanners. A rectangle popped up on her side of the main viewing window. Two green dots slowly blinked toward the center dot, *Khunda*.

"Ali, open a communication feed to both the Guard ships."

Ali pressed a button on the navigation console. "Communication open, Captain."

Lexy sat straighter in her chair. The Guard members wouldn't be able to see her, but the small change in posture gave her confidence.

"This is Alexandra Greggs, Captain of the transport ship, Khunda. We do not wish you any harm. We have learned about the Council's use of undercover Guard members in the attack on Aria. Khunda and her crew were fighting against the attackers."

The silence filled the void as they waited for a response. The comms crackled.

"Captain Greggs, we have orders to take you into custody for the attack on the enlightened planet, Aria."

"Did you not hear me? We were protecting the people of Aria," Lexy shifted forward in her seat, her hands gripping the console, "Nala Brevil, once a member of the Guard, led a small crew in the attack on Aria. We were there under orders from the Council to locate former CTA security officer Apaleo –"

"We know your involvement with the criminal," the Guard member interrupted, "We have orders to use whatever means necessary. Give up now, Lexy." His voice changed to pleading. "Please."

The man's words stunned her. Z gasped, then slammed his fist on the console button to mute their side of the communication.

"Lexy, is that Captain Cassen? What the hell is he doing out of retirement?"

Lexy slid her hands down her face. "They think we won't fight if they send people we know."

She reached over the console and unmuted their side. "Captain Cassen, we don't want to fight you, but we will if necessary."

"I'm sorry, Lexy," Captain Cassen replied before cutting the connection.

Lexy dropped her head.

Z huffed, "Well, that's a load of shit. How many years did we work for and with that ungrateful–"

"That didn't sound like he had a choice," Apaleo interrupted.

"You think the Council is holding something over his head?" Trent asked.

Lexy relaxed her grip on the console. "I think Apaleo is right. I don't believe he would attack us without something being used against him."

"The file transfer is done. We're good to go, Captain," Ali said, her voice holding regret.

Lexy could guess that Ali had been excited at the opportunity to study the high-tech ship, but she knew just as much as Lexy that without days, if not weeks. It was too much of a risk. It took time to ensure there weren't any traps in the ship's systems. Their only option was to destroy it so it wouldn't attack any more innocents.

Lexy sighed, "Z, ease us out of the cave. Trent, charge to full power and fire as soon as we are out of the explosion's range."

Nora walked onto the bridge, nodding at Lexy in confirmation that she had finished packing the jump ship. Lexy pointed to a second fold-down chair next to Innes. Nora glanced at Apaleo before taking a seat and buckling herself in.

Z flew *Khunda* out of the cave and toward space. "Okay, newbie, we're out of range."

Lexy watched as Trent, now connected to *Khunda's* weapons system, focused his eyes on the hologram screen that appeared across his face. A streak of light traced their course back into the cave. Dust and debris burst from the cave, causing a ripple effect on the moon's surface.

They didn't have time to watch the aftermath as the Guard ships headed straight for them.

Z pushed the engines, and *Khunda* sped into the darkness.

"Don't go straight to the jump station. Let's take them along the scenic route," Lexy suggested as Z maneuvered *Khunda* through a long-forgotten battlefield.

This section of the Virgo constellation was a dead land, filled with floating pieces of warships from a final battle in the Grey War. They weaved between chunks of rock and metal. Silence on the bridge only added to the eerie scene. Lexy rubbed her hand along the edge of her chair, the smooth, cold surface grounding her to the realm of the living.

A high-pitched beeping and flashing red light drew her eyes to the console.

"Alright, Z, they are entering weapons range. Time to lose 'em," Lexy commanded, trying to keep her voice steady.

"You got it."

Z slid his palms along the console's surface, guiding *Khunda* around tighter turns and faster direction changes. Shards of old warships jutted into their path. What little light the local sun gave off cast shadows from the left. While darkness swallowed everything it could from the right. Two flashes of light passed *Khunda's* right side.

"They're firing," Apaleo called.

"Yep, we see that. Hold fire until I say so," Lexy commanded.

Three more flashes zoomed past the left side of *Khunda* before the whole ship jolted forward, telling Lexy one of the shots made contact with the outer energy field.

Lexy leaned forward. "*Khunda*, damage report."

"The blast lowered the outer field by thirty percent. No surface damage is detected," *Khunda* answered.

Z chuckled without looking away from the debris field. "Glad I pushed for the power grid upgrade after the Royal mission, huh?"

Khunda jolted to the left. Lexy narrowed her eyes at him. "Less cocky, more flying."

Lexy waited as more shots flew past the bridge's main window—another jolt.

"Alright, that's three. Start firing back, but keep your charges low. I want them to know we don't mean them harm." Lexy entered commands for *Khunda* to shorten her scanner range and redirect power to the outer field. "*Khunda*, what is our power field status?"

"Outer energy field holding at fifty percent, Captain."

Lexy turned to Ali, "Can you scan those ships and tell me how many crew members they have?"

Ali turned back to the navigation screen and began tapping icons. She shook her head, "Not at this range. We need to be closer."

Z grinned. Lexy didn't like that grin.

"You got it," he replied.

Lexy pushed back into her chair, "Tighten your seatbelts, everyone. This is going to get scary."

Lexy pulled the straps across her chest tighter as Z gunned the engines and flipped *Khunda* around to face the Guard ships.

"Ali, be ready to scan as soon as you're in range," Lexy called.

Ali entered commands into *Khunda's* system. "Ready when you are, Z."

Z steered *Khunda* at the Guard ships. He was playing chicken with them, and Lexy knew he wouldn't give in. Lexy watched as the space between them grew smaller. The second, smaller ship shifted its course to the left.

"Fire at the second ship's right wing. It looks like they are redirecting power to their weapons. Their field will be weak," Lexy commanded.

Trent and Apaleo began firing. Energy pulses traced the path, connecting with the ship's wing. After the first few pulses hit the ship's energy field, small explosions told them they had made it through.

"Stop," Lexy sat forward.

She wanted to disable the ship, not to destroy it.

"We are in range. Scanning now," Ali called. "The main ship has five life signs, and the second has four."

Why so few?

Lexy didn't have time to find an answer, as *Khunda* was still on a collision course with the main Guard ship.

"Z," her voice was tight.

"I got this."

"Z."

"I got this."

"Z!" she yelled as the Guard ship pulled up at the last moment.

Z steered *Khunda* under the belly of the Guard ship. "Lex, I said I got this."

Lexy took deep breaths as she dug her nails into the armrests. Z flew out of the ship's range and turned *Khunda* to face its rear.

"Fire at its rear thrusters," she called out, trying to keep her voice from shaking.

Energy pulses connected with the ship's thrusters and small explosions told them they were disabled.

"Ali, what's the status of both ships?" Lexy asked.

Ali scanned the ships. "Both are disabled. A transmission was to the nearest Guard station. They're dead in the water."

"Suck on that," Z hollered.

Lexy released her grip on the armrests. "They can still fire, so get us out of weapons range and then celebrate."

"Oh, yeah," his hands began sliding around the console again. "There we go. Out of range."

"Good." Lexy pushed herself straight up in the chair. "Ali, open a direct message to both ships."

"Ready, Captain."

Lexy summoned all her confidence, "Captain Cassen, I can't make this any clearer. We are not your enemy. Both of your ships are disabled, and we could easily kill you all, but we won't because we are not the bad guys. I don't know what they told you, but if it made you attack us, it's a lie."

Silence.

Lexy looked at Z, who shrugged.

Ali spoke before Lexy could, "I've closed the line. Lexy, Cassen is sending an encrypted message."

Lexy looked back at Ali in shock.

"Play it."

A video message popped up in front of them. An older man with blonde hair and pointed ears stood in what looked like the captain's quarters. His eyes were creased and tired.

"Lexy. Z. I am recording this as we depart the Guard station under orders to find *Khunda* and neutralize her at all costs. Seeing as where the order came from, I can only guess that you have found yourselves in the middle of this war for power," Cassen sighed, his forehead wrinkled. "Understand that I didn't want to do this. My hands are tied. They control everything. If I don't comply. If I don't keep my mouth shut." He dropped his head, rubbing his temples. "Lexy, I knew your parents. I trust their judgment." Cassen's head lifted and his blue eyes seemed to look straight at her. "Finish their mission."

The feed went black.

"I didn't see that coming," Z snorted.

Lexy's mind began racing. This went much further than she thought, and far more people knew about it than she could imagine.

"Z, get us to the jump station. We have to go."

Chapter Seventeen

Lexy's boots met the grass. Her shoulders sank lower as she sucked in the fresh air. Hints of blooming flowers and soft rain reminded her of spring on Earth.

Lexy touched the comm in her ear, "How's it look, Z?

"It looks clear. We don't have any Guard on our tail, and the closest life signs are miles away."

"Good." She turned and called into the cargo bay. "Let's do this and get out of here." Lexy hurried back up the ramp.

After disabling the Guard ships, they made two jumps to get to this planet. A small rock with a tiny population of farmers. This was where Apaleo had a contact that could get them to the rebel lab.

I guess if you want to hide under the Royal's nose, this is where you go.

Trent fell into step next to her, heading toward the jump ship. "Ali and I stripped the jump ship of all beacons and markings. It can only be recognized if someone hacked the core, but Ali is sure that would be impossible. She wrote some unhackable code."

Lexy hid her smile. Ali really was a genius.

"If she says so, then I believe her," Lexy said, taking the comboard Trent handed her.

She reviewed the changes to the jump ship's navigation. Z had added all of the unregistered jump stations so that Apaleo,

Nora, and Innes could travel safely. Lexy sighed. It was time to go their separate ways. She should feel relieved, but the weight of their unknown future began to settle in. Lexy pushed the worry from her mind. If she stayed focused on the tasks in front of her then she could keep the fear away.

Trent, Z, and Ali agreed to return to Earth to regroup. Lexy felt unsettled as if they were just going to wait around for the Council to decide their fate.

Nora and Ali said their goodbyes as Innes rechecked the case in which she had packed the samples and journal. For her, those were now the most precious items on all of the enlightened planets. Her small frame carried the weight of so many lives; their lives.

"Let me help you carry that," Z called to Innes as he joined them in the cargo bay.

Lexy stopped Trent to watch as Z carried the case onto the jump ship.

She elbowed Trent. "Remind me to talk to him about this when we get home."

"You mean mock him?"

Lexy shrugged, "Same thing." She looked at Trent's face. He was smiling at her. "What?"

"Nothing," he shoved his hands into his pockets, "I just can't wait to get home."

Lexy nodded in hesitant agreement as she headed toward the ramp to the jump ship.

Apaleo came to stand on her other side.

"Everything is ready, Captain."

"Good. Not to sound rude, but you should leave before something new finds us."

Apaleo nodded. "I agree. The Council seems to have an issue with us."

Lexy giggled. "Was that your attempt at a joke?"

Apaleo shifted into motion, walking up the ramp. Trent and Lexy exchanged looks of confusion as Nora stepped in front of Lexy.

She took Lexy's hand in both of hers. Nora touched her forehead to the back of Lexy's hands. Lowering their head, unguarded, for even a moment was the warriors' way of showing gratitude.

"Thank you for being the captain I was always told about." She moved to stand in front of Trent, who stiffened. Nora wrapped her arms around him in a hug, causing his eyebrows to rise. "You are a warrior, and warriors must shoulder the pain so others may live without it."

Tears burned at the corner of Lexy's eyes as Trent returned the hug and smiled. Nora released Trent and joined Apaleo.

Innes and Z were talking quietly on the ramp.

Oh, I am so going to annoy him about this.

Trent cleared his throat to get their attention. Their grey cheeks turned red, making Lexy's heart just a little lighter. She watched Z live the party life, constantly worrying that he wouldn't find love. Maybe Innes would spark the need to have deeper connections.

Innes gave Lexy and Trent a small wave before moving to stand next to Apaleo. Lexy took in the three figures. Their lives had crossed, and they were all on new paths because of it. Lexy slid her hand into her pocket, wrapping her fingers around a small data crystal. Eyebrows pinched, she pulled the crystal from its hiding spot.

Without looking at it, Lexy moved up the ramp, her hand outstretched to Apaleo. His stern face relaxed as Lexy explained, "The rebels have taken over the news feeds when they killed Royals. Maybe now they can use the feeds for good. I think it's time for the beings under Royal rule to hear the truth. Your people deserve the truth, so I figured I would start with what happened to us." Lexy sighed, steadying her voice. "What happened to Marcus."

She inhaled deeply as Apaleo took the crystal from her.

"I will make sure your message is heard," he assured her, his voice soft.

Lexy nodded and joined Ali, Trent, and Z, who had moved off to the side of the bay so the jump ship could take off. Innes gave one last wave as the jump ship's engine began to hum, and the loading door closed. *Khunda's* floor vibrated under their feet by the propulsion system's frequency.

Ali wrapped her arm around Lexy's shoulders, leaning her head on Lexy's. Z slid one arm behind Lexy's back and leaned against her other side. Tears slid down Lexy's cheeks as grief tightened around her heart. They watched as the jump ship lifted its landing gear, turned, and eased out of *Khunda's* cargo bay. The hum faded, and the small ship disappeared.

Lexy was the first to speak, "I never thought I'd feel worried for Apaleo."

Trent chuckled. "Are you sure it's not worry that he'll come back?"

Lexy smiled. "Well, if we do ever see him again, you are my witnesses that I give Z permission to shoot him with the dart gun again."

"YES!" Z pumped his free arm in the air.

They all laughed. Lexy could always count on her friends to find humor in uncertain times.

Ali raised her head. "Z?"

"Yes?"

Ali sighed. "Get your hand off my ass."

✳✳✳

Lexy straightened her CTA uniform, letting her fingers slide over the two stars tacked to the collar. If she was going to do this, she might as well look like a captain. Lifting her chin, she reminded herself that what she was doing was more important than a third star. Tightness tugged in her gut. She had wanted to be a three-star captain for as long as she could remember, but now she didn't feel the same drive or need to fulfill that dream.

Clearing her throat, Lexy pushed the red dot on the screen. It turned green.

"My name is Captain Alexendra Greggs. I am a two-star captain for the Central Transport Agency. Many of you have heard stories about my crew and me lately. I want to assure you that that is what they are. Stories."

Lexy forced her hands to relax at her sides.

"We were thrown into the middle of events we had no knowledge of before the Council cornered us into hunting down a former Royal Guard member. No doubt they sent a standard civilian transport crew to hunt down one of the highest decorated warriors in all of the Royal planets because we were the best option," Lexy paused, her anger rising. Sarcasm dripped from her words. "It couldn't be because the vote to destroy the Grey planets is being pushed before the Council rather than going through the courts, as a ruling of this nature should."

Lexy's hand raised to stroke the stars on her collar. Her eyes lowered in thought. Before she knew what she was doing, she removed the stars and looked at them in her hand.

"My parents died protecting their cargo. They were honored and praised for it. But no one had ever told me the cargo was a young girl. No one told me she was around my age. That she was an orphan and one of the greatest minds any planet had ever seen. No one said she was on the verge of cracking the Ancient Blood code," Lexy raised her eyes and looked straight into the screen, "We found the warrior. We did what the Guard and Royal Guard couldn't. And along the way, the Council sent undercover Guard members to attack the Utu tribe on Aria, so the Council could blame us while we fought alongside those warriors protecting their homes. Their children."

Lexy closed her fist around the stars.

"They sent retired Guard members, against their will, to capture us for crimes we did not commit. Crimes we are being blamed for. In the course of these attacks, Captain Marcus Xetha was murdered. One of the best captains I have ever had the pleasure of working with. Killed by a ruthless Guard member that I turned in years ago for using her authority to harm civilians."

She cleared her throat, taking a deep breath before continuing, "I know many of you will choose to resist this information and turn a blind eye to the actions taken by members of the Council. But for those who are willing to ask questions and look beyond the box of comfort used to distract you– the rebels are not your enemy. The Grey planets are not your enemy. We are not your enemy."

Lexy slid the stars into her pocket. Her heart filled with understanding.

"I will hold hope that all of us can find truth without hatred. Without anger. Because that is our true enemy, rotting each of us from within. The Council is not at fault. Members of the Council are. Just like every king and queen do not rule the same, each person is responsible for their own choices."

Lexy smiled. Her heart was lighter somehow.

"How will you choose to live your life?"

Lexy touched the green dot. The recording ended. Her finger moved to hover over the button that would transfer the recording to a memory crystal.

Am I doing the right thing? What if this makes no difference?

Her finger waited for her decision. Her choice. Then, like an echo ringing in her ears, she heard the answer.

How will you choose to live your life?

Lexy pressed the button.

Ancient Blood Trilogy

Ancient Blood

Book Three

About the Author

Kristina Bak is a Georgia-based author of science fiction.

While in college, she began writing her first novel, *Khunda*. In 2016, she attempted her first NaNoWriMo. In 2017, she completed *Khunda* with the love and support of her NaNoWriMo family.

Now, her writing thrives within local critique groups and the writing community.

In her spare time she enjoys ice dancing, yes Georgia has ice rinks. Kristina lives with her husband and son.

You can find out more at KristinaBakWrites.com